attemptations

Copyright © 2011 Kim Clark
01 02 03 04 05 06 16 15 14 13 12 11

All rights reserved. No part of this publication may be reproduced, stored in a retrieval system or transmitted, in any form or by any means, without prior permission of the publisher or, in the case of photocopying or other reprographic copying, a licence from Access Copyright, the Canadian Copyright Licensing Agency, www.accesscopyright.ca, 1-800-893-5777, info@accesscopyright.ca.

Caitlin Press Inc.
8100 Alderwood Road,
Halfmoon Bay, BC V0N 1Y1
www.caitlin-press.com

Edited by Meg Taylor.
Text design by Vici Johnstone.
Cover design by Pamela Cambiazo.
Cover artwork by Kelly Louise Judd.

Printed in Canada on recycled paper.

Caitlin Press Inc. acknowledges financial support from the Government of Canada through the Canada Book Fund and the Canada Council for the Arts, and from the Province of British Columbia through the British Columbia Arts Council and the Book Publisher's Tax Credit.

Library and Archives Canada Cataloguing in Publication
Clark, Kim, date
    Attemptations : short, long and longer stories / Kim Clark.

ISBN 978-1-894759-66-3

    I. Title.

PS8605.L36229A88 2011   C813'.6   C2011-904934-1

attemptations
short, long and longer stories

KIM CLARK

Contents

Dick & Jane and the Barbecue	7
Split Ends	12
Mr. Everything	16
Lucky Strike	25
Flickering	28
Tangled Threads	32
Aphylaxis	36
Solitaire	
Lillian Lillian Lillian	43
Lillian Shadow Lillian	49
Shadow Lillian Shadow	66
Shadow Lily Shadow	74
Lily Shadow Lily	78
Lily Lily Lily	83
Six Degrees of Altered Sensation	
H̶H̶H̶ H̶H̶H̶ 11 Days of Xmas	93
Chicken in Mourning	107
Cougar Sighting, Siting, Citing	129
Dar-Win-or-Lose-ling Techno Love	148
Liberation	157
Acknowledgements	174

Dick & Jane and the Barbecue

PROPANE SAFETY

> *Propane tanks have a multitude of connections: valves, gauges and other attachments that look interestingly complex.*

Dick and Jane were uncomplicated strangers, and then they weren't. They were casual acquaintances, and then they were friendly acquaintances, and that's how they remained ... in public.

They each went home alone—Dick to sleep with his epileptic dog, Rusty, and Jane to her microwaveable foot warmer even though it was May on the west coast of Canada, all hummingbirds and blooming dogwoods. They went home alone because their kids were grown and distant and their marriages had failed to live up to the North American dream. They went home alone because they were both past their prime, Jane even further past than Dick, and because failures wreak havoc on acceptability and desirability in social encounters of the third kind.

They each went home alone until one night they didn't. After Dick's multiple advances outside her car and Jane's adamant refusals inside her car, they ended up in private. And in private, they became friends. With benefits. And soon-to-be-disclosed baggage. And loneliness, which unleashed a lot more than Rusty, left at home with his seizures.

The visible parts of the propane tank play a vital role in the usability and serviceability of the gas tank.

They were seized by the mutual and unquenchable need for human touch in every way, shape, and form—all fingers and lips and whatever else they could find. You can't beat Stop-Swap-'n-Go fornication, they decided. But even a long night is only so long. Jane said goodbye. Dick said he'd call. Jane said no, it was just a one-time thing. Dick raised his eyebrow, kissed her nipple, and went home to Rusty.

The second time, failures were revealed. Jane's failures included multiple undefined marriages and an obscure disease involving physical wasting, which she couldn't always conceal, especially in private. Dick's failures and wounds were salted away, revealed only in the light of day—the serpentine scar along his thigh, a pair of healed punctures near the shoulder blade. Proof of violence, even before the rest of his story came out: a cracked-out ex with a knife, a mention of AIDS. (But we just! ... Dick, with sweat still on his lip, said no, it's okay, he'd been tested.) Dick's disclosure had something to do with honesty. Jane candidly repeated that a relationship was out of the question. Her privacy was at risk, but she couldn't resist ruffling his hair before he left.

The inside of the OPD valve is engineered to only allow propane in or out if the internal valve is depressed.

And so, there was a third time. And it was so ridiculously fine, that is, until Jane flailed around the kitchen, spilling morning coffee, and said that was really enough. They couldn't go on bangin' their brains out all over the house. Dick asked Jane where, then, did she want to do it. Jane said in the car. One last time.

Jane refused Dick's subsequent publicly discreet offers to "keep her company." Jane, with too much time on her hands, was leaving town. California, she said, a holiday. Dick, with a shutdown at work and too much time on his hands, asked when. Jane said in three weeks. She told Dick he needed to find himself a woman. A real one, for a real relationship, in a real world.

> *Some propane users take it upon themselves to paint their tank a colour that complements the colours of their home or deck. This presents a safety problem. Propane tanks need to reflect heat, not absorb it. The absorption of heat creates the possibility of a high-pressure situation.*

Sitting on the end of Jane's bed, he said, I could get lost in you. Don't, she said. There's no map in or out. But Jane had a sudden impulse, an irresistible thought—limitations make endings tolerable, at least. Let's be seventeen for three weeks, she said. Then it's over. Dick agreed. With everything.

Dick and Jane allowed themselves the luxury of time, spent it together, usually naked, every chance they got. Flaws and failures, having been dragged out into the open, became as irrelevant as the clock. They were insatiable. They were funny. They were "only seventeen."

> *An important point to note is that under normal operation, a propane regulator will make a humming noise. This is normal.*

Midnight phone calls, afternoon siestas, and seventies music prevailed. They swapped tunes. Jane rented movies—*A Clockwork Orange* and *Shaft*. Dick played his guitar, "Stairway to Heaven." Jane ordered take-out, two days of food at a time. She sang under her breath.

At the end of the three weeks, they said light-hearted goodbyes (Jane breathing a sigh of relief). Have fun, they told each other.

> *A saturated vapour contains as little thermal energy as it can without condensing.*

Kim Clark

And they did have fun separately. But it wasn't the seventies anymore, so they emailed sporadically. Dick talked dirty and sweet in his emails. Slept near his computer awaiting lackadaisical responses in his cool basement, shoving pills down Rusty's epileptic throat. Jane sent photos of a cheese factory in Tillamook, a sunrise in Carmel, the Golden Gate Bridge. She always asked, had he found that woman yet?

> *Most will rightfully argue that the LP regulator is the heart of any propane gas system.*

There was a message on Jane's phone when she arrived home. Dick's voice said, call me. And then another. So she did, and before she knew it, he was at the door. Dinner, he announced, proffering steaks, mushrooms, home-made potato salad. Jane supplied the wine, but it was an awkward affair. No comparison to the seventies. It's a fact that you can never go back, and Jane's theory was that you can never go forward. Regardless, they carried on.

The day Dick brought over the shiny black portable barbecue was as hot and dry as Jane's throat on seeing it. Oh no, Jane thought. It was horribly domestic. He'd even brought a small table to set it on, old graffiti almost obliterated. I'll do everything, Dick said. I like doing things for you. Jane almost gagged at the thought of after-dinner dishes, she and Dick side by side at the kitchen sink. They ate dinner together in near silence. Take the barbecue home, Dick, Jane pleaded. I don't need it, won't use it. Can't tolerate it, she thought. Dick ignored her request and left the following morning without it.

> *The connector actually allows the regulator to be installed closer to the service valve.*

Jane pondered the barbecue from across the patio, then examined it more closely. A greasy grey film had spread across the dark lid. Its folded chrome legs had tiny chips missing. The rotund propane cylinder, rusted in several patches, had a curled and torn label attached. *Superior Propane*, it read. *Stop-Swap-'n-Go*.

Jane stewed. Dick went off on a camping trip to clear his head. He'd mentioned his upcoming birthday before he left. Was she expected to do something special for the occasion? They were on the verge of falling into something mundane and predictable. A never-changing forecast of hot and dry, rather than intermittently warm and moist.

Still, when Dick called, Jane answered. Then he showed up one Saturday after midnight, unexpectedly. A little drunk. A lot late. You're all blue, Dick said, reaching for a breast. Jane said, yes, looking down at the skimpy cobalt chemise.

When Jane called the day before his birthday and again on his special day, his voice mail said unavailable. Fine, she thought with a sense of relief.

> *Regulators have internal moving parts that are subject to wear and tear. They are not repaired or subject to repair: they must be replaced.*

Three days past Dick's birthday, Jane called again. A little drunk. A lot late. And he finally answered. Did you get your birthday blow job, she asked. Silence. Dick said he'd been meaning to talk to her about that. Silence. He'd met someone, he said. What took you so long, Jane asked. You can keep the barbecue, he said. Excellent, she said. Dick.

> *Propane regulator connections come in varying lengths and angles. Always use caution.*

Split Ends

It happened on the first day of spring, a day flirting with the promise of summer. Sun triggered a craving for a good book to read on a beach, or a bench, and pushed me through a sweet, late afternoon down the hill to the small library. The stacks were quite empty. I found myself facing the Bs, my back to the Fs, in a super-naturally infused oblivion, memories in disarray, attempting concentration.

The conscientious layer of my brain was looking for a book, simple as that. It was a book by the Australian-Canadian writer Jonathan Bennett, *Verandah People*—a book about water, and a distance-dissipating tactic to connect me to my daughter living in Perth on the Indian Ocean.

As my eyes scanned sections of titles by letter, name, category, another cerebral layer acknowledged the divisions we construct in remembering our own histories: before we moved to BC, when I was thin, with my third husband, before I had kids. My eyes still followed the order—Bansford, Barnett, Barrington, and I noticed most spines on this shelf were beige, white, a few blue or red. I remembered a bookstore that divided books by colour to achieve a yellow wall, a red wall. The experience became a visual-literary adventure, full of pleasure and surprisingly good finds.

I reached for a bright touch of turquoise, pulled it out. The author's name was my own maiden name. Having no brothers or sisters, I half-wished it was a mystery cousin—some thread of attachment to literary fame or insight into my family heritage. The book was a pleasant size, the worn cover still lovely, an abstract silhouette of a woman's neck and shoulder, pale peach, and the barely hidden outline of a face just turned away, tips of long hair grasped in her hand to be examined. The title read *Split Ends*. The author's first name was the same as mine.

I searched the back for more information. There was a photo. It could have been a younger me but with shorter hair than I have ever worn. "Well researched, quietly compelling, sharply observant" was a quote from the *Winnipeg Free Press*. Another said "A story about coming of age in the heart of the Canadian Prairies and the exquisite bonds ..." A crease in the cover obliterated the rest.

I flipped to the bio for clues. She was born in my hometown of six thousand people. I thought, just for a moment, that someone had stolen my story but realized, of course, I had no story to tell. She had graduated from the University of Manitoba and spent years up north in The Pas and Flin Flon, revelling in the North. Well, that was definitely nothing like me. There had to be a rational explanation.

Sinking onto a three-wheeled step stool, I moved into the chapters, flipping, reading snippets, searching simultaneously to connect and refute.

"Five minutes to closing," I heard someone call out. The air was heavy, still, expectant.

I mentally snatched landmarks and descriptions randomly from the page and the scenes constructed were the history of my memories, impossible for anyone else to display with such intimate clarity. This author spoke with the experience of comfortable familiarity about the details of a life that had been mine.

In Chapter One I read about a prairie winter, tongue touched to a frozen doorknob, could have been any kid's tongue but with striped mittens knitted by my grandmother. Then on through an anxious scene of blizzard driving, wipers pounding against mesmerized front seat muffle moving endlessly into the white-streaked tunnel of night outside Winnipeg.

In Chapters Three and Four she wrote of fishing in frigid lakes for striped perch and heftier pickerel. There was the naive joy and satisfaction of bait fishing; hauling up the tiny four-pointed nets bulging with the flash of a hundred sleek minnows, two hundred hook-target eyes heading for the family freezer. I could hear the crunching demolition as we marched over thousands of resigned fish flies drifting across the road, only a few left to flutter in your face or hang in precarious clumps on the street lights downtown. The clincher for me was an episode of getting a hook caught in my sunburned ear. Yes, it was my ear. And my freezer. And my crunching feet. I claimed them for my own.

But in Chapter Eight we shared nothing I recognized. Later in the book came strangers and a hint of despair. The split must be in the chapters between.

Now I have always been curious about the choices rejected, the paths not taken and the events and repercussions left in the wake of our small existence—the split ends discarded while one hair continues to grow only to split off again. I half expected the book to disappear into the too-warm library air as I heard the voice again, "The library is closing." Clutching the book, I approached the front counter.

"Have you read this?" I asked, holding out the turquoise book to the librarian, half hoping for recognition. But she was ready to go home. She took my card without seeing me.

"Yes. There are others, as well. But we really have to close."

"I think this is me ... was me. It could have been my life."

"Maybe mine too," she laughed. It was a flip answer, refusal to engage, while the clock was running.

I was too confused to explain. I felt anchorless. I wanted the other books too. I had to get some air.

"I'm sorry. We really do have to close. Enjoy that one though," she said as she ushered me out the door. A low-sun cool made me shiver as she continued, "It's the last she wrote before she died. She was only thirty-one."

Mr. Everything

If I tell you it was the truth, I would be lying. If I call it a lie, I'd be hiding behind some truth. But I will tell you that there was a quiet uneasiness in the weather that first day, a blood-stirring taste of spring sun. The clouds on the horizon pushed the idea of thunder toward me as I walked past a cluster of fuzzy prairie crocus and on up the long gravel drive. Even the solitary blackbird, streaked red, held his tongue. The driveway veered off, disappeared behind a large shed on the left. An old Bronco, maybe a '66, sat up on blocks next to a rusty Volkswagen with a flat tire. Past that was a large garden, waiting for the attention of a rototiller, then a slim stretch of bright lawn. I thought about turning around. It looked like no one was home. I reconsidered, decided to leave my business card—Mr. Everything. I needed the extra money—No Job Too Small—if I was ever going to clean up my life. I followed the curve.

The house was large, a shambly place that had once held promise, I would guess. A pair of huge budding maples snuggled close to the faded siding. Bright reflections of sky in the upstairs windows paled the structure, gave it the patina of dusty uncertainty.

She sat in a lawn chair, a pale dark-haired woman with a sweater balled up in her lap, narrow straps of a yellow dress slipped off her shoulders. She was enjoying the warmth, eyes closed in relaxation. She was not beautiful, you have to understand, but that picture in my mind has made her so.

"Hello," I called, not wanting to startle her but doing just that. "The gate at the bottom of the driveway was jammed."

"Oh, hello." She straightened, adjusted her straps and pulled the sweater on. "You must be Mr. Everything." She took a long look, a reading.

"That's me. My business name, at least—a jack of all trades. I go by Brett. Brett Cawston. I can take a look at the house. See what exactly you want done and what exactly I can do for you. On the phone you just said it needs work."

"Yes, and you said you'd be here today. Of course." She clipped that shoulder-length hair up on top of her head. "I'm Ruth Vandermeer." And she reached out her hand to me, a warm delicate hand missing half its baby finger.

That's when I first saw the gun—its small size not diminishing its power—on the table beside her. I shook her hand as she glanced to the weapon, then held my eyes as she slid a newspaper over it.

"Been getting in some target practice?" I asked, wanting things out in the open. I thought about the damage that compact pound of metal could do.

"The crows ... " She waved behind her to the clothesline—a man's plaid shirt pegged by its tails, a jigging bra, pastel panties, a thin white nightgown. Pillow cases gestured, flannelette sheets lifted slightly, lightened earlier of their water burden into the afternoon sky. "I guess I could show you the house."

"Sure." I turned and moved toward it. "Outside or inside?" I sensed her eyes on me but no movement.

"Just wait. Um, I have a list somewhere ... here it is." She was not frail exactly but hesitant around the edges like a midnight moth. "Hey, actually, why don't you just go ahead and look around."

"You don't want to show me then?"

"You don't really need me. The list will do the trick. Go ahead.

I'll be right here. The sun's almost gone. We can talk about money when you're done."

So I nodded and made my way around the outside of the house, agreeing with the list for the most part. Yes, it needed paint, had a couple of cracked windows, some rotten railings on the front porch. I took some measurements, jotted notes about what I'd need first. She had made it sound like a done deal. We'd see.

I called, "Should I just go on in?" But she didn't answer, waved me ahead, so I did—a stranger in a strange family land. The list was vague regarding the interior.

The door was sticky, the knob loose. There were shoes just inside, those skater shoes kids wear with the laces loosely tied, and boots, their steel toes revealed through worn leather, a man's denim jacket and winter coats on the hooks. The kitchen was impersonal, not a cozy territory. No salt and pepper, no teapot on the table. No African violet on the stained windowsill. I found the broken cupboard door, the torn lino, a series of burn marks, dark halos on the countertop next to the stove.

Every tap in the place leaked, the kitchen and both bathrooms. Two large holes stared back at me from the drywall where a towel rack must have been. Rough spackle patches on the kitchen ceiling looked like the beginning of a repaint that never quite got off the ground.

The upstairs bedrooms told a little more of the family story—looked like two boys, grown, maybe gone now, and a husband ... somewhere. A husband who slept in the master bedroom with his wife, his slippers at the foot of the king-size bed, his and hers bedside tables, no pictures, a dresser with a missing drawer. A green garbage bag sat in the back hall, half-full, a broken armchair lay tipped on its lifeless back in the room meant for living. One door just off the kitchen was closed, locked.

I shook my head, puzzled. I waited for a label to come to mind, like wealthy folks, good people, or flat-broke-see-you-later. I could usually read the customers pretty well and pretty quickly but here something was missing.

The sun hovered between the treetops and the thrust of edgy cloud as I came back out. She hadn't moved much, just shifted around with her feet on the ground. I shut the door behind me on the colourless interior, stepped toward her small warmth.

"It's getting cool," I offered. She seemed nervous about the sky, hurried me into the conversation.

"What do you think? About the house? The job, I mean. Can you do it?"

"Well, I can do it all, depending on money and time."

"I have a budget."

"Well, I have an hourly rate. This kind of work tends to uncover more problems as you go. But I can give you a price for the exterior paint, lumber, and then go from there. Are you thinking of selling?"

"Yes, that's it. Selling. I ... we just can't manage all the work. When could you start?"

"I do some pipe-fitting here and there across the province. Almost a seasonal thing, so I have chunks of time for these jobs. Carpentry. Plumbing. Whatever."

She cut in: "But when can you start? Soon?" The first raindrops were making her panicky. "Oh, it's later than I thought. Just call. Let me ... us know when."

"I can start tomorrow, pick up paint. That'll take about a week. It needs some scraping." I felt like I was doing something wrong, keeping her from something. "I'll call you tonight with a price, if you like. Will your husband be around? I'll need a hand or some scaffolding for the highest parts."

That threw her, I could tell. "We'll figure something out." Then she drew the mask back on, composed herself, ignored the rain.

When I pointed out she was getting wet, she agreed, covered her head with the newspaper, and sent me on my way.

I looked back only once. The clothesline was beginning to droop while she sat unmoving in the rain. Maybe the job wouldn't be straightforward. Maybe I'd lose the number. I picked up the pace, made a run for the truck and pulled out before the first lightning.

But I did make the call as soon as the storm had blown through. Talked myself out of paranoia looking over the estimate, the decent profit without gouging anyone. I'd have my own downpayment together soon. The forecast looked promising, painting weather.

She agreed to the price, said go ahead with the job. Tomorrow'd be fine. Just get what I needed. I had an account at the building supply place. She picked a heritage colour, bland grey but dark enough to cover. It was an unusual way to do business, but what the hell?

Everything about the outside work was as smooth as could be expected. I hired a high school kid to help out the first weekend for the grunt work, scaffolds and unloading. Then I worked my way around the house. The weather held long enough for the paint to dry. I made progress on the Vandermeer place, a real difference if you ask me.

But it was like working for ghosts. I'd leave my hourly bill each Friday in an envelope stuck in the door. And every Monday morning I'd find an envelope in the same place, with a cheque signed by Ruth. Sometimes there was a note saying she was away or thanks for the great work. The door remained locked, the curtains closed, but always a radio on somewhere in the house. It was easy this way, no chitchat, no interruptions.

It was a Friday I finished up the last of the trim and started dismantling the framework. The truck would pick it up tomorrow. I broke a sweat, stripped off my shirt, enjoying the work, the strength and sureness of my body. I grabbed a beer out of the cooler in the pickup, cracked it, and poured it down my throat with the kind of gusto you only find in solitude. I opened a second bottle, sat back in a lawn chair to admire my work. The work of *Mr. Everything*. Nicely done. Next week would come the inside, fiddlier work, less satisfying. I wrote a note saying I'd need access to the house for Monday, added my hourly bill. I tucked the envelope in at the door like always. But, not like always, there was a sound. The turn of a lock. The door opened ever so slightly. The envelope fell.

I hesitated, stuttered "Hello?" I even knocked, pushed the door inward. "Anyone there?"

It was Ruth's voice, saying, "Come on in. I'm in the kitchen."

"Hello, Ruth."

"Mr. Everything." Ruth said. Just like that, as though it were true. She was sitting at the table with a full drink in her hand, a little drunk maybe. Jeans and a T-shirt, nothing sexy, but her hair was loose, messy, a hint of wild. There was a pretty full bottle at her elbow, another empty glass.

I felt awkward, sweaty. "I didn't know anyone was here."

"Barely anybody. Just me. Have you got another beer? Or would you prefer whisky?" She gestured with the glass.

"I was just on my way. Really."

"Take me with you." She laughed soft-like and looked away.

All I could think was to get out and I could have walked, but no. There was an urgency about her mouth. Pleading. Trouble. So I pulled up a chair next to her.

"Yah, one drink. Sure. It's been a good week. The paint looks good, eh? What do you think?"

"I think," she said, "it looks very good. I hardly recognize the place. A good thing. So ... your beer or my whisky?"

"Yours, I guess."

She poured a generous portion into the waiting glass. She'd been ready for company.

I was edgy, curious. "Is your husband happy with my work?"

"Carl, you mean? He hasn't seen it. He's living up in Fort Mac."
"Oh. Permanently? On a contract or ... ?"
"Permanent avoidance, actually."
"Avoidance?"
"Of me. The house. The way we aren't and the way I am now."

I'm drinking fast and don't want to hear this stuff. Complications. "This is getting kinda' personal, Ruth."

"Personal. Yes. You have no idea."

And then she switched up, apologized for making me uncomfortable and all that, the way women do. We talked about the plumbing then, the interior of the house. She refilled my glass. I could talk carpentry and shit forever.

All of a sudden, out of the blue, she leaned in, placed that mouth of hers against mine. I'm a sucker for soft lips. I'm a sucker, but cautious.

"Ruth, I really have to go. This is not a good idea." And I actually got up out of my chair.

"Just, wait. I ... need help."

"Whatever help you need, I can't do it. I'm a carpenter."

"You're a man, Mr. Everything. You rebuild things."

"Houses, Ruth. I work on houses."

And then she said it. That she's a cripple. She's lame. It was a dirty trick, the timing, but it worked well enough to sit me back down. She told me about the accident, the pain, the way her life had slipped away, her boys grown and gone, her husband distant. She never cried or anything. I kept saying, you don't have to explain all this. I had to ask how she managed and she said, badly, slowly. There was a wheelchair, two canes. She was lonely, awkward, undesirable. She was broken, needed a fix, which made me laugh a little. Christ. I wanted out but couldn't find a way and then it was too late.

It was Ruth's turn to say it. "I have to leave. And don't know how." She kissed me again, really kissed me. How could I say no to all of that?

We fell into a rhythm over the next month. I worked my way through the inner rooms. She was there in the house, in the wheelchair even, as though once I'd seen her naked, felt her arms and lips and slept against her skin, her scarred and damaged body, it was all out in the open. She talked about leaving and so did I, but neither of us ever said the word "together." I could be her courage for a little while but love never entered into it.

The job was almost done. We knew it.

We sat on the front steps, me with my tools already packed up in the pickup. Ruth looked at the crows winging past the roof into the summer sky, not at me, saying, "I have to get out of here, leave before I can't."

"You've been saying that since I met you."

There was nothing I could do, after saying these words, but walk away. Again. The prairie stubble is still there, star-nosed moles digging through the rows, celestially pink, pale asterisks nudging through the top layer of earth. I know this as I kick through a riff of gravel, a clump of loose hay. The chickens scatter in complaint. This woman makes me crazy, makes me hate her, want her. It feels like an endless script. A bad script. Mr. Everything. Right.

"You will never leave! There is nothing I can do for you!" I yell back toward the place I picture her, probably sitting in that damn lawn chair by now, a murder of crows scattered in the maples. I continue crunching down the drive, talking only loud enough for myself now. "You will never—"

The shot startles me. I turn automatically. Start running back. I'm thinking, if she isn't dead, the second blast could be for me, for what I have that she doesn't.

I wish I had not gone back. I wish I could remember her the way she was when I first laid eyes on her, sitting in the spring sun, thin straps, bathed in yellow. She was waiting for me, the first blast a fading echo as I rounded the shed. She placed the pistol in her mouth. Slowly squeezed the trigger. Everything in sight and out of reach.

Lucky Strike

Cheryl's younger brother, Ray, had relapsed. He hadn't hung onto his remission or either of his wives, just his two boys.

"Cancer's back," the oncologist said. "High-dose chemo and radiation." So they grabbed onto that hope. Cheryl organized her girls, Ray's boys and all the family and friends they could muster and began living a different life.

For Ray that meant months at the Cancer Lodge, isolated, sicker than sick. Months of his kids seeing less of him while needing more. Grandma Dodie set herself up to spend time with Ray and spell off Cheryl. And for Cheryl life became yo-yo limbo, travelling the ferry route between Ray in Vancouver and the balancing act at home. To heck with the *Survivor* show, this was the real thing for each of them.

By the time the cedars dropped their rich chaff and the mountain ash shed their vivid leaves, life for Cheryl had definitely taken a turn. Her job at Canadian Tire kept her and her two girls alive and kicking, not very high sometimes, but kicking nonetheless. They'd just have to manage with a bigger household. There was no mortgage on her small rancher. Thanks to a lapse by her tight-fisted ex.

The stubborn coolness of the October morning and the late ferry irritated Cheryl, even more than the chaos at home. She felt apprehensive about Ray's condition. She dreaded those bad days.

The helpless feeling was overwhelming, the tiny treatment room oppressive.

Rolling down the window, she gave a wry smile and mouthed "Hi" to a neighbour, while noticing the jerky movement of a one-legged grey gull. She drove tiredly onto "The Queen" yet again and, following the snaking line of brake-lit vehicles, pulled into the outside lane of the lower deck.

Cheryl turned off her car, pulled up the emergency brake and allowed her eyelids to fall shut just for a moment. She breathed slowly. She was relieved to have the luxury of not talking or thinking or being strong. She could hear gulls bickering on the nearby railing as the vibrating hum of the huge engines quickened. And that was it. She was gone.

If anyone had more than glanced into that green station wagon, they might have wondered at her absolute stillness. They might even have wondered fleetingly at the faint smell of lilies-of-the-valley or ripe raspberries. Although not gone from this world exactly, Cheryl was certainly gone from her present state and situation.

She sensed hints of lavender and licorice, childhood smells. Cheryl saw the scent of raspberries, felt chimes and heard smiles. Quick memories flashed, bright baby faces, jewelled noses, laughing wrinkled cheeks. They kept coming—the soft sighs, dreamy eyes, colours, shadows, warm breeze, cool water. She felt strange, good but definitely strange. Discumbooberated, Dodie would say. Was she all right? Had she had a stroke? Passed out?

She raised her hands and looked at them, moved them, then checked the mirror. She was well acquainted with the mussed hair and aging face, but what the heck was that by her eyebrow? Eeeeuw. Her brain registered the slightly open window splattered with bird crap and the stickiness by her left temple, just as a deep male voice made the "approaching Horseshoe Bay" announcement.

A quick swipe with a tissue and except for a little tingle she was as good as she was going to get.

Off she went along the Upper Levels Highway, through Stanley Park, down Georgia, Burrard and finally 10th Avenue. There was the Cancer Lodge. The smokers huddled at the entrance were hard at it. The irony wasn't wasted on Cheryl. A small chuckle escaped. Where did that come from?

Cheryl managed to talk Ray into getting out for a short walk and some pretty fresh air. They shared pot pies for lunch, cut his toenails, talked about their funny kids and their mum, Dodie, and that was a big day for Ray. He looked exhausted as they hugged goodbye. More than three hours had zipped by. Damn. She'd forgotten to mention the seagull incident. Her brother would have gotten a kick out of that.

Back on the ferry, she walked to the railing for a moment. It had been a good day. Silly to worry. Cheryl turned back toward her car, just as ... swoop ... would you believe it? If it wasn't that damn one-legged seagull, and he got her again. Only this time she remembered the sensation precisely. Weird! What a crazy day. She felt great!

That bird had dropped some serious soul substance, more potent than chicken soup, meditation or tranquilizers. It was better than the time travel Cheryl had loved to read about as a girl, better than her daydreams or vivid night dreams.

Wait a minute! She scraped the crud off her face and onto the rim of a hurriedly emptied water bottle. This was like a stress vaccine with a short shelf life. She could try it on Ray, she thought. Her mind was full of plans. Could she market it? Sell it? Maybe be rich? Famous? Help the suffering world? Possibilities. Yes! Even an ordinary woman is perfectly capable of entertaining an extraordinary dream.

Flickering

Frances made her way, broom in hand, across the front porch, always sweeping from the top down. Step by step, day after day. Then she cleared the path of cedar bits, seeds and chaff. Clean and simple. She kept order along the sidewalk all the way to the front gate, regardless of weather, most satisfying now in the fall when the maple and elm slough off their small chaos, when the storms disguise the proper pattern of things. Her neighbours think her effort heroic.

A small two-door pulled up to the curb. It was the paper lady with the local gazette.

"Hi, Rose." Frances leaned on the gate for a moment.

"Morning," Rose said cheerily, stepping out of her car to hand Frances the rolled paper. "You're early this morning."

"I am. Couldn't sleep."

"I know what you mean. My old man's always wakin' himself up snoring. He wanders around the house. Me, I never hear a thing. Hey, that reminds me. If you hear of anybody who wants to take over my route, let me know, eh? I'm starting work at Walmart next week. It's not a bad route, about three hundred deliveries."

"I wish Rob would take it. He hasn't been able to find anything since the mill laid him off. I'll mention it."

"Sure. Let me know. Well, I gotta go. Only half done." Rose stooped to pick up something that caught her eye and held it out to

Flickering

Frances. "Is this yours? Need a flick o' your Bic?"

"No, but it may belong to one of the boys. Thanks." *Boys, gawd, would they always be boys?* Frances slipped the blue lighter into her jacket pocket, decided she might as well burn some of those leaves. Rose waved as she got back in her car.

Frances loaded up the wheelbarrow and headed around the side of the house to the barrel. She arranged the leaves, a bit of paper. The small flame from the lighter caught the edges, grabbed. The first smoke was not unpleasant.

She heard a car door out back, then the rev of the Mazda. John, her oldest son, leaving for work. At least he has a part-time job. He had screwed up his marriage, was back home now. Rob had been out of school for a couple of years now but had never really left home. Frances knew how hard it was to find a decent place, enough money, but they should be out on their own, regardless. She should be on her own, needed to be on her own. *The two of them, perma-boys. What a pair.* Things seemed to be slipping in all their lives lately. *Jesus, I just wish they could get it together.* Together.

Frances had pictured their futures as separate, some orderly independence, following a tidy plan of small successes. She had always managed to get by, to provide for them. Polite organization. Relentless purpose in the face of challenge was becoming the challenge, her dreams a disturbance, her imaginings restless. She was aware of a slight tic below her right eye, a small muscle out of control after another sleepless night. She held her fingers against her cheek to quell the small spasm, sighed, and straightened her back. What could she do but encourage them for a little longer.

She parked the broom, got a mug of coffee and sat down to read the news, jotting a quick note to Rob about the paper route, wishing he'd get himself out of bed and do something, anything. There was one article that was worth a reread. The old Sample place up on the hill had burned down. The volunteer fire department had been undermanned, had been unable to save any of the wooden structure. They needed to recruit. She added to Rob's note the phone number at the fire hall just down the street. Encouragement.

She had been surprised at the enthusiastic conversation about the note. Well, half of the note. Rob had smirked at the idea of a paper route but both boys had pounced on the volunteering idea. They'd walked down to the fire hall, talked to the chief, filled out applications and begun training Wednesday nights. They seemed happier, the house was running a little more smoothly. They had their uniforms, their beepers, some self-esteem even, looked like the good men she had imagined they would grow to be.

Now if only she could sleep. She started walking in the evening, a little farther each time. It seemed to help a little. There was a certain satisfaction in the renewed familiarity of the streets, a closed gate, a newly painted fence, an old Dodge pickup finally gone, spirited away to someone else's territory.

She enjoyed the boys' stories about the practices and their first few small blaze experiences. She read all their instruction manuals, procedure packets, fire prevention info. She was happy knowing the safety procedures were strict. Because their home was in the same block, they were often the first to respond to the call, to start up the trucks. Even the fire chief, Al Farley, had mentioned to her at the post office just how well they were doing.

Frances's walks became cathartic, first through the neighbourhood, then farther and farther into different areas of the sprawling town. She noticed the immaculate yards and the capped chimneys, more steadily smoking now in the early winter evenings. She even called in a chimney fire out past the park. Her sons didn't like her walking at night but she was cautious, always took her cell phone. She'd been glad she'd had it that night.

A younger woman was doing the paper route now. Frances didn't care for her, too chatty, tried to avoid her by sweeping early

Flickering

or late. But the woman, Bonnie, had a brother, a fireman just like her boys. She told Frances one day that he'd been promoted to Assistant Fire Chief, a real paying job. He was such a hero, Bonnie had said. He deserved it. The paper that day had an article saying the fire department had been busier than usual with the colder weather and so many woodstoves going.

Frances started to notice an alarming number of fire hazards, not just in carports and backyards, but in the downtown area. Dumpsters overflowing with cardboard, electrical cords draped through construction sites under wood and debris, plastic containers of solvents. The newspaper reported a suspicious blaze over on Greerson Street. Arson was suspected. *No wonder*, Frances thought. *People just aren't careful enough.*

By February there had been a few more suspicious fires. The old library had burned down, too, started by a cigarette, they thought. Rob and John were really getting into the workings of the investigations, were feeling pretty cocky, enjoyed being part of the rescue team although they had yet to rescue anything more than a dog. But the folks who lost their garage put a nice thank-you in the paper. *And he's got two job interviews. Maybe with his name in the paper, he'll get lucky.* Frances thought about freedom and solitude. *Maybe I'll give up the house, get an apartment. Alone.*

In March, there was a fire across town, one of those tall new houses under construction, another behind the convenience store. Bonnie came right to the door to show Frances the front page. There were her sons and two other men in their gear rolling up hoses in front of a smouldering heap. Their names lit up in her eyes. She couldn't wait to show them. She put on her jacket, still damp, fingered the lighter in her pocket for luck and headed out with her broom to clear the chaos of last night's storm.

Tangled Threads

Two men walked along the quiet street, choosing the broad expanse of even pavement over the sidewalk. The younger man, Nathan, wore a ball cap and long shorts, giving a youthful edge to his thirty years. His Uncle Nick sported silver hair and worn Nikes. They were on a mission to find some good, cheap books and check out the view from the tower, before they said goodbye to each other and to Nathan's childhood home.

Nathan had been staying in his mother's house since her sudden death a month earlier, trying to come to terms with the loss and the legalities when his mother's brother, Nick, had offered his company. Here they were, a few days later, renewing a tenuous relationship, sometimes enjoying it, often feeling strained by the eruption of emotion.

They had shared schnapps and stories about Adela amidst her belongings but it wasn't until the walk to the library that Nathan began to reclaim the intense details of life with his mother.

"You know, Nathan," Uncle Nick spoke slowly. "You'll be alright in time."

Aware of the lightness of the gnarled hand resting on his shoulder, Nathan wondered aloud just how he would ever feel alright.

"You will gain strength from this loss but slowly. Adela shared her spirit with the people whose lives she touched. Each and every one has inherited a thread of her essence to help them gain strength of spirit. Some will feel the tickle of a colourful thread as they chuckle to themselves over a joke shared in youth. A practical piece of string might show itself as Adela's handwritten recipe in someone's cookbook.

"I think of my sister," Uncle Nick went on, "when I hear the gawdawful screech of an E string on an untuned violin. She had a bad ear."

Nathan smiled just a little.

"Your bequest is like a thick coil of strong rope," Uncle Nick continued. "You may not ever see that rope but if you shut your eyes you can feel the strength of the rough fibres in your hand and the rope will be there. Grab onto that rope in your mind and just remember. So many memories twisted together ... you are fortunate to have had a mother who loved you and left so much thick rope. Just remember—and I'm talking about you now—don't leave a tangled mess, and don't trail too much black thread."

Nathan remembered another April day. There had been a late snow, not unusual in the eighties, but spring had burst through the crusty remnants and presented a fine day of surprising warmth. Purple-barked plum trees waved pink blossomed branches and crocuses crowded the steps. Nathan thought he heard a hummingbird whir by his head as he took in the day with all his keen ten-year-old senses. From the high front porch he enjoyed the regular Saturday morning routine of his neighbourhood. Spring was here and the possibilities of the day stretched before him.

His mother, Adela, called from inside the house, "Nathan, come to the library with me. They have the big book sale today. Maybe you can find a couple of books for yourself and you can help me carry home mine." Errands and chores. He didn't want an old book, just his freedom. It was never a request with her, just a statement, another expectation. Surely his mum was not going to steal his day, not this new bright day. He stayed where he was on the top step, watching his neighbourhood and wishing he was already somewhere else, biking to the duck pond, maybe, or warming up his ball glove at Hackett Park.

Nathan watched Mrs. Solinski let out her calico cat Fatima, who stretched and rolled before sighting a fat robin worthy of a slink and chase. Mrs. Dicksen shook out her rugs. Mr. Handel picked up the broken oyster shells left on the road by the hungry seagulls and replaced the puzzle pieces of broken Mermaid Street pavement kicked aside by the Gardener brothers on their way to the corner store for smokes. Then out the door came his mother, empty mesh bags in hand. Mother and son walked toward the library without speaking.

A tangle of turquoise wool trailed across the overgrown lavender by the church. A crow had been pulling at it but flew to a nearby tree as they approached. Nathan plucked the wool from the dry stalks and stuffed it into his jeans pocket, turning his back on the noisy crow. He sensed his mother watching him. He felt mean but was too stubborn to relinquish the wool or his day. Adela kept walking.

They approached the flat-roofed library on Trail Avenue. The four steps down to the door gave the narrow building a stooped, cave look. As well as the bulging shelves, tables of saleable books crammed the dim interior. He wouldn't look at the books but stayed outside, kicking stones into the garden.

"You are SELFISH with a capital 'S' and you will get CHORES with a capital 'C.'" His mother's voice had been icy as she shoved the book bag into his hand.

"Now that we've seen the old library, let's go to this beacon of a tower and that fancy new library of yours and find some treasures, eh?" Uncle Nick's voice had taken on a lighter note.

Nathan had lost the conversation. He had stepped into a memory incredible in its ordinary pureness. He was happier to wear the patchwork truths of his relationship than a saintly cloak. Uncle Nick seemed unaware of his confusion and laughed out loud at a swallow struggling with a tangle of bright yellow thread.

Aphylaxis

Almost quitting time at the Tan 'n Man Salon, she thought, and there is no freakin' way I'm stayin' late, not even five minutes. Keeping an eye on the door, Nadine reached up into the display case, moved aside a few bottles of lotion and slid the inconspicuous mirror aside. She lifted the small camera from the recess, rewound its film, and replaced it with a new roll. Lydia, her boss, would have to find someone else to do her dirty work after today—dirty but profitable for Nadine.

She tucked the film carefully into her hefty shoulder bag and studied her sculpted Deepest Plum fingernails from behind the pine counter. The overpowering smell of acetone and Tropic Tan had given her a headache. She'd had too much coffee and not enough breakfast, and if she didn't get out of there right at four, she'd be late for her class at the college. Medical Terminology.

Nadine's extended fingers led her eyes out through the window, across the street to a short woman with chopped, greying hair leaving Jimmy's Fish & Chip Shop. This small woman, a neighbourhood regular, manoeuvred along the Broadway sidewalk, keeping close to the roughly protective downtown buildings. She listed to the right despite her metal cane, cradling her fish dinner, its newspaper wrapper still clean. She passed the Money Store, Colour Your World, and stepped into the nearest crosswalk, coming closer until

she disappeared into the plate-glass reflection.
Aphagia, inability to swallow. Nadine recited aloud, a commitment to memory for the upcoming exam. *Aphemia, loss of speech due to central lesion.* This was the last semester she needed to finish up her course. If she could get there on time for a change and manage to pull off a decent grade on this exam, she'd land the medical transcribing job in Edmonton or maybe at Foothills in Calgary, union wages, benefits, all that. *Aphonia, lack of voice due to chronic laryngitis, hysteria or disease of the vocal chords.* She chewed her bottom lip, staring down the clock. *Aphrasia, inability to use connecting phrases in speech ...*

The woman in the crosswalk glanced down at her chest, checking for the plastic HELEN nametag from the thrift store. One of the workers had given it to her, jabbed it through a clump of her floral dress and knitted vest. *Helen, yes, right.*

Helen's speech hadn't been clear since her stroke the year before. *Aphrasia, the doctor had called it—without phrase.* But she had phrases in her head, all right. Complete poems from a distant, dead father. They just couldn't make it past her lips. *Chapped lips the colour of clay, baked, parched at the end of the day, torn, worn, shredded, frayed.*

Helen's voice was low and rough. "Shit!" was the only clear word she spoke with enough sporadic urgency to force pedestrians out of their closed-face, dead-eyed crowd consciousness to glance back at her, uncertain, before resuming their paths with renewed intent.

But right now, in this moment, walking down a late afternoon sidewalk in early summer, there were some certainties. She knew her small cheque was safely in the bank. She knew for a fact that the deep-fried fish and chips she carried home had a big enough smell to satisfy her hunger. The pleasant feel of heat through the newspaper wrapping was comforting against the inside of her arm and would help to ease her painfully slow route home. *Quit dodderin' you old fool, you!* "Shit!" she nagged herself, butting into her own string of utterings. She liked to be home before the shops closed up and her territory revealed its edgy personality, magnifying her vulnerability.

"Crap on a stinkin' stick!" Nadine said to no one but the towels, borrowing a euphemism from her twelve-year-old son's repertoire. She'd already wiped down the two tanning beds and cleaned up the half-moon detritus from the nail bar. She turned out the lights, hoping the next client wouldn't show up before she made her getaway. She'd warned Lydia. Nadine had made it really clear. She'd told Lydia she had to leave on time today. No matter what. Lydia had said, "No problem," but she still wasn't here. Nadine flipped the Open sign to Closed, then dragged the $19.99 Pedicure Special sandwich board in through the door. When the hands of the bamboo clock hit four, Nadine set the security alarm.

"Crap on a stick!" She had cracked one of her sculpted nails. She scooped up her mountain of books and bulging bag. With a hip check, she swung the door open, startling the mousy little woman who appeared almost beneath her.

"Geez," Nadine muttered, getting control of the door, letting it close.

"Shit!" growled the woman, trying to keep her balance, seeing only a streaked, bronzed Amazon bursting into her sidewalk space. They were caught flailing for an instant in an awkward shuffle.

"Shit! Shit! Shit!" Helen clutched at the brick wall, the woven bag, the woman, her dinner, her cane—anything to keep herself upright. Then just as suddenly, they broke apart.

"Sorry!" Nadine steadied the stack of books with her chin while turning the key in the lock before the freakin' alarm went off.

Helen caught her breath. She barely noticed the vague apology tossed her way but was struck by the artificial smell of tropical sweat and the shapeliness of the ample calves squeezing between crowded bumpers and disappearing behind the broad side of a large rusted van.

Nadine shouldered her books through the driver's door and onto the other seat, then climbed in. She willed that old woman's eyes away with a blast of Bif Naked's "I Love Myself Today" as she started up the engine and pulled into traffic, almost believing it.

Shaken, Helen muttered. As she collected herself, a slight movement on the ground drew her focus away from the loud lurching van. A roll of film bounced over the edge of the curb. Helen awkwardly made her way across to the now empty parking space, picked up the film, and dropped it into her oversized pocket.

By the time she reached the doorway of her rented room, she was panting with exhaustion. She collapsed into her dilapidated swivel rocker, her precious dinner in her lap. She wiped her damp chin and lifted her aching foot onto a small stool. While adjusting her vest around her, she felt the film and retrieved it from her pocket. Her fingers also found the forgotten silver-rimmed magnifying glasses. Earlier that afternoon, she had wandered through London Drugs and at the pharmacy counter had impulsively dipped into a box of magnifiers marked Please Donate to the Children of Africa. She had dropped the glasses guiltily into her pocket. Now she set the glasses on her nose and the rescued film on the peeling windowsill beside two rolls of her own. Helen lined up the three identical rolls of film, a trio of photo-soldiers standing guard against the sun.

Maybe her nephew Buddy would find time to develop them for her. He had his own darkroom. After all, she had taught him the art, the beauty of the captured image. Years ago now. She had nothing left to offer, no voice to explain. It took so much effort just to ask him for a favour, to communicate at all.

The sun shone through the small window in hot dusty streaks. She sighed, slowly rotating the old rocker, shifting her view over walls covered in faded newspaper clippings and magazine articles. She had been a pretty damn good photojournalist out east, award-winning even.

Nadine nudged the van into the bridge lane, almost tasting the certainty after years of living without it—a good chunk of money in the bank by tomorrow. It was time for some serious karma. Things could work out for her and her son, Gary. They would definitely get out of the dirty basement suite, get a better vehicle, get the hell out of this dirty city. *Hold on Nadine, you're not there yet.* Just one more thing to do, one last nasty.

She would drop off the film at that creep Buddy's right after the exam and get the final set of pictures back to Lydia in the morning. *Aphrodisia, extreme or morbid sexual passion.* Disturbing as it was, it had been worth it. She'd get her money and be gone. No more Tan 'n Man, no more Lydia, no more pictures. She was sick of the scam. Tired of Lydia's weird clientele. Friends, Lydia called them.

Helen's life had been so clear, so black and white. Now her black had faded and her white had yellowed and what remained was a palette of greys to infinity. Later, she realized she had eaten and forgotten to enjoy the fish. She rubbed at the bridge of her nose, setting the glasses on the windowsill. Surprised by the vivid colours of the sun through their refraction, she took several minutes to jiggle a pinpoint of brightness over her favourite Trudeau article.

The tiny rainbow looked obscenely out of place in the dust of lengthening shadows. At just the right angle, Helen could aim that beam at the pile of greasy newspaper lying abandoned at the foot of her chair. If she kept the rainbow still long enough, she could smell smoky traces of that palette of greys. Out of the

Aphylaxis

corner of her eye she noticed the films and was reminded of the pounding of her heart after the door incident, the near fall. She wondered about the other woman and what would be on her film. The Cambie Street Bridge? A poodle under a palm tree? Her terrifying fingernails? And she wondered if there were any worthwhile images on her own film.

The final had gone pretty well, Nadine thought, going over it in her mind as she pulled off the campus parking lot. *Aphylaxis, absence of immunity.* She reassured herself just a little smugly. It was clear sailing, light traffic down the hill to Buddy's place for the last drop-off. Only one red light—always a good sign.

Nadine clicked on her signal and smiled to herself as she waited for the light to change. Reaching over, she felt around in her bag. Found the familiar corners of her cigarette package, her lighter, her wallet. But where was the film? She turned on the interior light. Her frantic fingers ploughed through the bag. Ow! Shit! A drop of blood near the end of her finger clashed with the colour of her broken maroon nail as she pulled an unfamiliar nametag from the bag. It read HELEN. The light turned green.

Solitaire

Lillian   Lillian   Lillian

Lillian awkwardly shuffles the deck of cards for another game—the point, to make order out of random, pattern from chaos.

red   black red   black   red

But who is Lillian? She is not a mother. She is not even a daughter for that matter. Not a wife—never has been. Or a lover—despicable thought—not even a liker of much. No longer productive, in the sense of purpose, work. Friendship, well, "failure to thrive" is the best description. Wait, that's not true. Old Harold Jenkins is a good neighbour—the only neighbour up here—respectful, although he's been away visiting family or something for quite some time. Never mind. He'll be back. And there's Judy, the woman from town who cleans for her, delivers her groceries, checks on her once in a while. No, that's not true either. Lillian does not like her. Judy is nosy but necessary.

People are generally a complication. Lillian likes her peace and quiet, her tiny garden, rhodos and bleeding hearts budding up, one or two tomato plants when the weather warms. She watches the six o'clock news out of habit. With political parties (champagne and confetti!), devastation, and nudity presented at such a rapid-fire pace and in such an inexplicable order that she can't possibly comprehend it. Suits, tatters, and skimpies. Nonsense is the new reality, it seems. She would concoct an equally ridiculous history for herself, but it would take such effort and make no difference to a damn thing anyway.

What is left of the real Lillian? A small sack of bones hidden under sweaters, layers, blunt practical shoes. No, a faded paper bag stained with angry arthritic red in all the wrong places, psoriatic patches, liver spots. She's no queen, either. So, no

Kim Clark

jack   ten   nine   ...   five   four   three

There is no crown except in the face cards, no foundation but in the deck. Fifty-two cards, fifty-two weeks in a year; four suits, four seasons; thirteen in a suit, thirteen new moons in a year. Three hundred and sixty-five Xs on the drugstore calendar, a list of the small chores of living. The patterns of existence are one thing, but the interminable time it takes to carry out each small chore—each movement would bore a young person into tomorrow. Tomorrow will be April. The first day, a Sunday.

clubs   hearts   diamonds   spades   summer fall   winter   spring

It is going by ... like that. Lillian would snap her fingers if she could force the knobby inflamed knuckles into action. Yes, it's spring. A pale sun, a fresh greening through the window. Not unpretty or without promise—for others. The ache in her joints should ease up a little with the warmer weather. She stares out into the new leaves of alder and maple, sometimes for hours, immerses her eyes in the motion of the abundant cedars sweeping down the sides of the valley, nudging the edges of the small town named after the evergreen trees. Cedar.

    Must she always wake up? She is in some liminal state, neither heaven nor hell. She wonders at times if she is a ghost, invisible to all around her. Depression is not a tolerable word and suicide is impossibly untidy. Things could be worse but just how, Lillian isn't sure, except in association with the words institution and hospital, lost in a phantom ward.

    She had been up early as always, after a decent sleep, considering the pain. She'd made the bed, cooked and eaten the oatmeal, washed the spoon, bowl, and pot, dried them, and put them away. She'd swallowed her meds, some of the uncomfortable stiffness relieved. One mustn't take the pills except with food. And she had checked them all off on her daily list.

morning
one green   one red   two large white   one small

She rested a bit, played the cards, won here and there. Then wrapping her coat tightly around her, Lillian tottered across the porch, leaning on her walking stick for support. She skirted the perimeter of the house, taking note of the snowdrops blooming, the robins dragging string and grass, the still-brisk wind. Shadow stretched on the top rail of the low split-rail fence. A voracious mouser, the cat had gradually moved in over the winter months. A tortoiseshell, a mottle of patches—apricot, cream, fawn, and black—rather fluffy, with the most innocent of faces. Shadow sharpened her claws, no doubt to ready herself for the next kill. Harold's double-wide trailer, just beyond, was still lifeless.

Oh, Lillian.

Take a nap. Eat a poached egg and toast for dinner. An apple. A two-meal-a-day woman. Watch the news, and, good grief, crass drivel that is meant to be funny. Then a show, a documentary kind of thing about superstitions—cats and rabbits and such. Talismans. Luck.

evening two blue   two large white   one small   one capsule

Waiting for the pills to work, and bed—another dreamless sleep—and another day down, she plays a few games.

red black   red black   day   black day   black day   night day   night

Three hundred and sixty-five is the number of nights in a year.

Three hundred and sixty-five is the sum of all the cards in the deck—if you include a joker. The queen of spades, that black bitch, refuses to show her face. Goodnight to defeat and to Shadow, wherever she is.

Good grief! What is this? A racket of cars and gravel so close, they must be in her head. A dream, and not a good one. But, no, her eyes are open. She can make out voices and there are lights shining through the blinds and, oh dear, it must be some disaster. Or emergency.

Lillian feels panic, hobbles on stiff legs to the window. She peers into the night, but it's an unusual night. People. Next door, at Harold's. People with loud voices. Men and women, maybe half a dozen, yelling directions back and forth. They seem to be moving things into Harold's, boxes and tables, which is better than moving things out, especially at night. They sound happy, busy. Lillian, on the other hand, feels ill and anxious. Should she call someone? The police? No. There is nothing to be done but check the locks on the door. As the noise dies down, she falls into a fitful and uncomfortable sleep. She dreams about Shadow, crushed under a tire just out of reach of her aching fingers.

Lillian has missed the sunrise, feels unsteady and sore. Oh, dear. A late breakfast. On hearing voices, she remembers the night, pulls her coat on, steps onto the porch, and sees a car and a couple of pickups on the other side of the fence, a woman leaning into the box of the truck. A plump woman in very short shorts and a halter top, revealing her tattoos: a bright bouquet of lilies trailing right down her back, a large Bugs Bunny on her left shoulder. When she turns, Lillian notices her bare belly, ample hips, and large bosom pushing out every which way. Bulging plastic grocery bags and a case of beer hang from her stocky arms. All that bare flesh and it is only March. No, April. April first. April Fool's. "Oh, hey," the woman hollers at her over the fence, all smiles in what some might call an open face. A friendly face. "I'm Dawn. Your new neighbour."

Lillian suddenly sees herself as Dawn must see her: decrepit, unkempt in a nightie and coat. Fearful. A big part of her wants to be unpleasant. She stutters out, "Where's Harold?"

"What?"

"Harold! Where is Harold?"

"Oh, gawd. Didn't you hear? Uncle Harold, he passed about a month ago."

"Passed where? What?"

"He passed on. Died. You know. Look, I have to haul this crap in. Everybody's waiting. I'll come over in a minute. Did you know him?" Dawn looks back over her inked-up shoulder. She waits for Lillian's response, shrugs, then trudges, hips jutting forward, into what was Harold's home.

"No!" Lillian can't believe this, any of this. She calls weakly after Dawn. "Yes. I mean I knew him. But, no. Don't come. I must go in. The chill. Tomorrow." Lillian hears shouts and whistles from the open door of the double-wide trailer. Hollering about death over a fence with a stranger on April Fool's Day is no joke. Dawn replacing the sunrise is downright ridiculous.

Lillian mutters, "Bloody hell," words that feel unfamiliar and strangely satisfying. She spots a tiny mouse body on the doorstep, moves to toss it away with her stick, but instead slams the tip into the furry body, crushing it. A little blood and crunch.

This is not a good day. It's already noon. Lillian has a headache. She no longer has the respectful Harold. She does have the walking stick he carved. The rabbit-shaped grip is sadly worn, another phantom. She hopes he's in a better place. But that Dawn, Harold's niece of all things, she is not respectful. She is ... she is something else, beyond the pale. And Lillian's new neighbour to boot. What is she to do? Mustn't think too much. Perhaps Dawn won't last long.

Perhaps she's just temporary. Lillian hopes all those other loud voices are not going to be living there, too. She feels nauseous at the thought of that.

This is better—oatmeal, dishes, medication, although a little off schedule.

~~morning~~ afternoon
one green   one red   two large white   one small

I must keep my wits about me. A few games will calm me down.

red black red night day night day black day night   day night

No, no, no. More cars arrive next door, some motorcycles. And the music is blasting. Not the smooth tones of Patsy Cline's "Crazy" or the high tremolos of those Emmylou Harris ballads that Harold liked to play. It's bloody rock and roll, without the roll, just rough low howls of sound, all thumping and pounding from the open doors and windows of Harold's—no, Dawn's—trailer. They have lit a huge bonfire in the backyard and are sitting around swilling beer and smoking something other than tobacco by the smell of it. It escalates over the afternoon, more people, louder voices, the odd bottle breaking. The booming music is rattling the windows, but she cannot stay away from the panes of glass.

Lillian needs to keep an eye on the hooligans. One of the men pees on her fence. The language is foul. She is sick with worry. Sick—that anxious knot in her stomach. She will need an extra pill tonight—and early.

evening
two blue   two large white   two small   one capsule

Lillian   Shadow   Lillian

The news is something else. Gabriola, Jedediah, Valdes—all nearby islands. What now? Lordy. It's feet, human ones, not in pairs, but detached single feet. Mostly left feet. Some of these feet have been found on local island beaches, they're saying, over the last few months. No explanation. *No explanation! Stop watching.* There are enough things to worry about without this. Local dismemberment, crude. *A talisman,* she thinks, *that's what I need!* An amulet, a charm of some kind. A rabbit's foot would be appropriate. She had one once. Where could she get one now? Tomorrow. She'll figure out something tomorrow. *Get hold of yourself. Go back to the cards. All fifty-two.*

black red black right black right black right left   right left

Close the curtains. Lock the door. No, open the door, just a little. Dawn's crew seem to have dispersed, no lights on, no vehicles. Good. "Shadow. Shadow? Yes, come in quick now." Lock the door. "Shadow, where can I find a rabbit's foot?"

fifty-two bones equal   feet   twenty-six bones   equal   foot

Lillian retires to the small comforts of the bedroom, tucks her new purpose away for the night and sleeps right through a dream and beyond—she, Lillian, fleet, small and low to the cold dark ground, agile as all get-out, walking, running, stretching. She cannot stop stretching, forcing her muscles apart, together, rhythmically, sometimes in tandem, making herself long or tall. What absurd joy in the nighttime body under a new moon.

    She hears a baby bawling intermittently outside. No, a cat howling and scratching at the bedroom window. Shadow. Lillian is confused by the haunting sound and the late morning sunlight peeking through the curtains. Too much time in bed often leaves her as stiff as an old board. But not this morning. She makes her way to the door, feeling quite good, not spry exactly, but definitely good enough to check into Shadow's ruckus. Lillian is sure she let the cat in for the night. Poor thing. Had she forgotten?

Lillian unlocks the door. And there is Shadow, but not alone exactly. The limp body of a young rabbit lies on the doormat. Lillian does not hesitate. She gives the cat a sharp glance and picks up the fluffy form, so beautifully soft, still slightly warm. Ah! As she turns to go back in, there's another bawling sound, but this is no baby. It's Dawn, spunky, smiling, and downright vulgar, climbing over the fence and swaggering toward Lillian.

"Morning!" Dawn yells. "Sorry, I forgot your name. You remember *me*, right? Dawn … from next door."

"Oh, I remember you." Lillian's not lying. There is the awkward predicament of the rabbit, dead in her hand, and again her dishevelment, and only in her nightie. Drop-in company is offensive.

Dawn goes on, rarely pausing to breathe mid-spiel. "Sorry about the noise over there. Did you even hear us? Nothing better than brews and pizza on moving day, eh? Yah, a bunch of my buddies helped out, ended up staying 'til the stereo was hooked up and the booze was gone. You know how it goes. Friends are great." She pauses and grins. "Even the bad ones. What's your name again?"

"Lillian."

"Whatcha doin' with the bunny, Lillian? Got a good recipe for dinner, or what? Ugh, gross. Sorry, I couldn't do it myself. Eat a bunny. But it's natural and all that, I guess. There are tons of them around here, eh? I'd rather get my meat plastic-wrapped, if you know what I mean." Dawn laughs, winks, but barely misses a beat. "So, I was gonna bring this bottle of sherry over that I found in the cupboard. Uncle Harold used to drink it, but I think somebody finished it off. So, yah, it was just to say sorry if we kept you up, you know, make peace or something. Unless you didn't hear us ... "

"I'm not deaf."

Dawn gestures to the rabbit. "But you're hungry, eh?"

"Are you married, Dawn?"

She hoots. "No fuckin' way. I like variety."

"What a surprise." Lillian's voice is brittle, imagining a string of roughneck boyfriends.

"You married, Lillian?"

"No, but I really should go ... "

Dawn's bare feet are slightly apart, planted in just the right position to block the doorway. More tattoos—a circlet of bright blue dots at the left ankle. Shadow slithers between those feet, then stops to lick the gaudy red of a toenail. Dawn shivers, jumps a bit, but carries on. "You know, my dad and Uncle Harold used to tie flies. You know, for fishing. Fly fishing. They used to use bunny fur for that. Used to preserve the skins and pick off bits. They caught a whack of fish. I never could hack the smell of them—the fish, you know. Gag me with a spoon." She gestures accordingly. "There's a book in that sherry cupboard. Some old homesteading kind of thing. They used borax to preserve them. Weird, eh? But it works for laundry. Whatever." There is a jangly tune from Dawn's back pocket. She pulls out a cell phone, opens it and smiles sweet and wicked. "Gotta go, Lillian. Hello?" She's already walking away, talking into the phone.

Lillian is alone with the rabbit. Finally. What to do first? Dress. Eat. Medicate. Get down to the business of attempted alchemy. Fly-tying and skinning.

~~morning~~ afternoon
one green   one red   ~~two~~ one large white   one small

The rabbit—quite miraculous in its luxuriant softness, the delicate bones within—causes Lillian only the briefest hesitation.

Luck. Magic. Call it what you will. Lillian knows somehow that for it to work she must be clear, purposeful. She needs to feel safely in control of her diminishing world, and the rabbit's foot could be the ticket to keeping chaos at bay. The practical side of things cannot get in the way of mystical progress, regardless of her lack of experience in butchery. But then again, even the word *abattoir* has a beautiful sound if she doesn't think about it too much. She has no axe or cleaver for quickness. But a kitchen knife would do the trick. The rabbit is so young, so fine.

The path around the side of the house, the side farthest from Dawn's, will have some suitable surface. This is not an act for witnesses.

Lillian holds the rabbit by its left hind foot, dangling the body across a fallen alder sapling. One slice is not enough. But drawing the blade across again and again, the body suddenly falls away. Some worthwhile things take work!

The foot is first and foremost on Lillian's mind. There is little blood, just a smear on her fingers. She carries it carefully into the house, dips the meaty end of the foot in the small container of borax, making sure the flesh is covered, and leaves it on top of the TV to dry out. An appropriate place, Lillian thinks. She washes her hands, uses copious amounts of lotion. Borax can be hard on an old girl.

Now I wait. And I play. And perhaps later, I will dream.

black   red   night   moon   right   left moon   light

It's been three days. The news is disturbing, the ads much the same. Little difference in their reality content. An emaciated fashion model in a raw bacon suit. A clip about schizophrenia, one of those support ads, sharing in paranoid suggestion. *This is the first scratch and sniff for TV. See the large blue dot on the screen? Scratch it. Smell it. What do you smell? If you smell anything at all, this may be a symptom* of schizophrenia. Call this number or go to www.something_or_other. She refuses to smell it, because of the proximity of the blue dot to the desiccating rabbit's foot. Lillian's no fool. She turns the sound off, leaving the images to flash.

It's been three days with no Dawn. Oh, she's around, comes and goes—out in the late afternoon, home at gawd-knows-when—but it's quiet at least. No dreams, either. No anything except the furry foot drying out nicely. Just a matter of cleaning off the crust of borax and re-dipping every day. The warmth of the mute TV should hasten the curing. Funny word, that—curing. This feels like progress, a different kind of cure as far as luck goes.

morning
one green   one red   one ...

A knock at the door. Then another. *Dawn? No! I will not answer it. She's calling my name.* There's a key in the lock. Blast. It's ruddy Judy.

"Just a minute." *Is everything in order? Why wouldn't it be? She's seen me at my worst.* "I'm—" But Judy's already in. Plain, tidy, pastel, slightly sour Judy.

"You okay, Lillian?" asks Judy, already slipping off her shoes. She has a bucket, mop, and bag of cleaning goodies. Pledge, no doubt. "You didn't answer."

She's looking from Lillian to her pills. This calls for a smile of some sort. Get-out-of-my-life reassurance.

"Of course. Yes. I heard you. Maybe you're the one going deaf." Lillian musters that smile.

"You sure you're okay?"

"Fine. Quite fine. It's the spring air, perhaps. Just go about your business. I may go for a small walk."

Judy's looking skeptical. "A walk?"

"Just a little one." Lillian scoops the pill bottles into the drawer, knowing Judy will sneak a peek, check the labels as soon as she's gone. "I may poke around in the garden."

"What's that funny smell?" Judy glances around. "Have you got mice? Maybe dead mice?" She's sniffing like a tracking dog trying to pick up a scent. Lillian wonders if she's smelling the ever-returning blue schizophrenia dot. *No! The rabbit foot! Lordy, I can't let her find that. She'll think I'm strange. Or guilty.*

"The place needs an airing-out is all. Leave the door open. I'll just get my coat." As Lillian talks, she manages to get around to the TV and palm the foot.

"You seem to be moving pretty well," says watchful Judy. "Maybe spring and a good airing will do you some good."

Lillian heads toward the door, her coat buttoned, a soft patch of luck now safely in her pocket. "Judy, what happened to Harold?" Lillian knows she'll know. The comings and goings of Cedar are the driving force of Miss Nosy-Parker-Judy.

"I thought I told you. Harold was heading out to Alberta, Bony River, just north of Edmonton. A family reunion, or something. Vonnie down at the post office told me. His car went off a bad corner up the canyon. Blew up and everything. No body. Sad, eh?"

Lillian nods, not surprised. Somehow it's better than knowing nothing. "Have you met his niece?"

"Oh, Dawn. Yeah." Judy rolls her eyes, slipping on her latex gloves. "She's a peach. Got herself a job bartending at the Cedar Arms, and that nice little property inheritance next door here. She's luckier than most, I'd say. People losing jobs left and right. The mill's been down for six months already, not good for the hubby. After twenty years on the job, he figured we were set for life, could just pension out. Well, things are damn tight."

Lillian can see Judy's going to ask for more than her ear. She's getting teary. But all she says, reaching for a bare hand with her latex, is "I'm so glad I've got my regulars, Lillian."

Lillian avoids her, mumbles about the walk, and is out the door. *I'll have to avoid returning for at least an hour or the conversation will be endless. Multi-purpose Judy, I would not want to be.* Neutral people take on the lives of others, glean shades of interest. Dawn, on the other hand—if she were a colour—would be a deep orange like the lilies tattooed over her back. Perhaps her colour is leeching out into the tattoo. *What a thought, Lillian. Really.*

"Ah, Shadow, you brindled lovely. You blend in night or day. A camouflaged huntress with flame-yellow eyes. What colour am I? There is no colour for invisibility, and that is what I'm becoming. Simply fading away. It's not right."

out   bland   in spring   Lillian   Dawn   Shadow   queen

Lillian stands a little straighter as she fingers the rabbit foot in her pocket. She makes her way slowly around the small yard, poking about at roots and soil, sometimes pulling aside the detritus of winter from erupting bulbs. She hears Judy running the vacuum periodically and reminds herself to keep her back to the windows and Judy's prying eyes. Lillian searches around the small alders for the rabbit remains but there is nothing but a few tufts of fur. Shadow sits nearby, yawns and proceeds to wash her face, claws retracted.

There is the startling snap of a twig and Dawn appears around the corner of the house. Lillian staggers a little off-balance with the sudden forceful presence of the young woman. She reaches for support, finds only Dawn's plump, very firm arm. Shadow bolts. Lillian rights herself, feels a slight tingling in her fingers. Human touch.

"Hey, Lillian. I remembered your name this time." Dawn smiles even as she talks. "You got company? I saw a car out front, and you out in the yard. Hey, I found that bottle of sherry. Wanna have dinner? Like, just casual, but something nice. I'm making something yummy. I actually found this recipe with a sherry marinade, so the bottle's not quite full. Here." She holds the bottle out to Lillian, assesses the situation—gnarled hands and a walking stick. "I can just leave this by the door. Who's here? Someone staying for dinner?"

"It's my cleaning lady. Judy. She'll be gone soon."

"Oh, great. So, whaddya think? Dinner at six? You're not vegetarian, are you?"

"No, definitely not."

"Oh, good. Cuz we're having meat. Well, chicken. In sherry. With strawberries. I only have frozen, but whatever."

Lillian readjusts the walking stick, wishing she had a talking stick so that she could control the conversation. "No. Dawn. Really, I can't do dinner. I have things to do."

"What have you got that can't wait 'til tomorrow? C'mon. It'll be fun. A few drinks, a few laughs, a little get-to-know-your-neighbour chit-chat."

"I don't see how I can ... "

"Aw, c'mon, Lillian. Get over yourself. I don't bite." Dawn bends over to pat Shadow, who has reappeared, sidling up to her smooth stocky ankles, her feet in a pair of flip-flops. Shadow, who has an aversion to Judy and her vacuum, is enamoured of Dawn.

Lillian can't possibly use lists or rest or solitaire as reasonable excuses. She cannot come out and say she is afraid of going out for dinner. Or that she's unnerved by Dawn herself. "Well, fine then." How bad could it be? Potluck bad? Undercooked chicken? *No, surely. It's just a couple of hours.* She can pull the fatigue card early.

Dawn's quick to respond. "Okay, great. I'll be over at six. I'll bring some beer, too. I'm not really a sherry girl."

"Oh ... dinner here?" *Lordy, lordy, lordy.* Lillian has lost control of the situation again.

"Yeah, didn't I say? My place is a freakin' pigsty at the moment. Maybe I should borrow your cleaning lady. Judy, right? Don't think

I've met a Judy yet."

"Well, it's inevitable in a small place like this. It's guaranteed *she*'ll meet *you*." Lillian realizes with these words that she wants to be done with Judy.

"Geez, is that a little warning there, Lillian?" Dawn raises her pencilled eyebrows. "I gotcha. See ya at six." And she's gone.

Lillian heads for the house, meets Judy on her way out. *Blast, there's the sherry bottle.*

"You're done already?" Lillian asks, attempting to keep Judy's eyes averted from the evidence. But, evidence of what, she thinks, a life?

"My regular two hours. Not much more to do really." Judy spots the bottle. "You taken up drinking, Lillian?"

"Heavens, no. I, uh, found it up by the road. Just litter, you know. Oh listen, it slipped my mind. I seem to have misplaced my house key, Judy. Would you mind leaving yours?"

Lillian waits while Judy digs in her purse for the key.

"Okay then, Lillian. I'll see you in a couple of weeks. And give me a call if you need anything in the meantime."

"It's not necessary. I'll be just fine, thank you."

Lillian will call Judy next week, during the day when she's sure to be out. Just leave a message. Avoid direct contact. She'll tell her it's the economy. A pension cheque only goes so far. Lillian smells only artificial lemons in the house, but it is a dustless and shiny clean. *Dawn for dinner!* Lillian is exhausted. It has already been a day.

Lillian   Judy   Shadow   Dawn   Lillian

What to do, what to do? First ... the calming cards. The surprising number of pairs that keep coming up is unnerving for the game of solitaire, nine follows nine, two follows two, over and over. And mostly red. Perhaps a rest. But sleep is elusive.

She'll set the table.

Lillian lays on a clean tablecloth, white, and two place settings of company china. She shakes her head. This is Dawn, for heaven sakes, hardly someone to impress. The good china is put away and replaced with her everyday dishes. She puts on a clean blouse, but covers it with her old comfy sweater, tucking the rabbit foot in the sagging pocket with only a small clump of crumbling borax. She cannot remember the last time she had company.

Two hours to go. She totters out to the corner of the yard, picks a few short branches of pussy willow, arranges them in a tall vase near the TV but changes her mind. She trims them down, putting the stalks loosely into a sealer and puts them on the table. Her heart is pounding with the effort. Panic. Has she taken her meds? Oh, now it's too late for the morning dose and too early for the evening dose. She'll re-adjust tomorrow. *One hour to go.* Back to the cards. Nothing but red. *Ridiculous*, she thinks, putting on the TV. *No!* The blue dot may show up.

Dawn arrives early, her hands full, banging on the door with her foot, calling too loudly, "Lillian! Lillian, open up or dinner'll be all over the porch instead of in our hungry guts. Come on!"

Lillian opens the door just in time to take the tipping casserole that is perched precariously on the open box of beer pressed against Dawn's barely concealed, generous bosom. By the time she's set the pan down in the kitchen, Dawn has cracked a beer, and surveyed the interior of Lillian's house, room by room. "Smaller than my place but tidy helps, eh?" She offers Lillian a beer, which she refuses.

"I don't drink beer, Dawn."

"Right. Where's the sherry then? You finish that off already?" she says looking around, checking the porch and sure enough finding it there. She reaches down between her breasts, pulling out a small book. Yellowing newsprint. "I almost forgot. Here's that book I found. You know. The fly-tying and fur stuff. Remember?" Dawn tosses the book onto the coffee table. "Lots of pictures 'n diagrams 'n stuff."

Lillian thanks her, frowning, and mutters about needing to sit down, and settles herself on the edge of the chesterfield, attempting to avert her eager eyes from the tattered book and its title—*An Outdoor Compendium*. She feels she is in the eye of a tornado. But Dawn appears oblivious, making her way through kitchen cupboards until she finds a tumbler, overfills it and plunks herself down next to Lillian, handing her the sherry.

Dawn holds out her beer bottle. "Here's to you and here's to me. May we never disagree. But if we do, the hell with you, and here's to me!"

Lillian has no choice but to touch glass to bottle. Manners. The sweet thick liquor is a rich surprise.

Dawn leans in, suddenly intent. Intent with questions, even giving Lillian time to answer, and sometimes ask back.

"How old are you, anyway?"

"I'm old."

"Come on. Eighty?"

"Lordy, no. Seventy, if I'm a ... "

"I thought you were older."

"It's the arthritis, I suppose, and life ... "

"Or lack of it." Dawn swills back her beer. Lillian sips. "What do you do for fun?"

"Fun?"

"Yeah, you know, like hobbies or travelling or, I dunno. I'm twenty-six, having a blast, not ready to grow up. Friends, parties. You know."

"Well, I read, play cards. Living takes a lot of effort," says Lillian, but she's kind of stuck on that number twenty-six. This young woman's probably already had a lover for every letter in the alphabet.

The conversation goes along, while Dawn replaces her beer periodically with a fresh one, refills Lillian's glass. Finally, she puts the casserole in the oven. The two women move to the table, Lillian sitting primly, properly. Dawn, slouching, reassures Lillian she won't have to lift a finger.

"You ever have a thing with old Uncle Harold?"

"A thing?"

"Yeah. A date. An affair? Maybe you were secret lovers, eh Lillian?"

"Good grief, no! Never. I didn't know him well. Although he gave me a gift once. That walking stick."

"He probably wanted to get into your pants." Dawn is grinning.

"Stop it. Really." Lillian flushes, tries to change the subject. "Harold was quite a carver. See the grip on the stick. The lovely rabbit."

Dawn looks briefly. "I never knew."

The stove timer goes off and dinner is served. A one-dish affair, not beautiful, but the chicken and saucy potatoes with peas and carrots are very tasty. Dawn clears the table, quickly stacks the dishes, plunks the last beer and the near-empty sherry bottle on the table, saying, "Gawd, relax, Lillian. You know what you need. A massage. You ever had one?"

"Heavens, no!" Lillian's panic is evident.

"It's not surgery! I hate doctors, hospitals. They'll kill ya. But this is different. Better. Just sit forward in the chair, lean on the table. Get comfy!" Despite Lillian's protestations, Dawn stands behind her, treating her once again as though she were a shadow, voiceless.

"Where's the cat?" Lillian asks.

"Must be out. I'll check in a minute. Relax!"

Dawn has her warm hands on Lillian's shoulders, working gently at first over her neck, even down her back. Lillian is relieved she's still wearing her sweater. It feels too, well, intimate. She imagines Dawn's hands on a man, one who'd already gotten into her pants. Lillian lets out a small sherry-induced laugh. More likely, she thinks, Dawn got into his pants.

"What's so funny?" Dawn asks, continuing her ministrations.

"Oh, nothing. Nothing at all." She was enjoying the massage. Muscles pushed and pulled, stretched in rhythm.

"You can pay people to do this for you, you know. For your arthritis. It might help. I get it done. I've got a real hunk for massages. Gives me a cheap rate for a little feel." Dawn laughs uproariously. "I'm kidding ya." Her cell phone rings. "There ya go, hon, all done." Dawn gives Lillian a final pat, then moves away to talk into the phone, kidding with someone, laughing, promising something or other in silky tones.

"I gotta go, Lillian. It's been a slice. You feelin' good?"

Lillian is now the one leaning, elbows resting on the table. "Lovely. Just lovely." She doesn't want to move just yet.

"That's okay, I'll grab my stuff and head out." And she does, shrieking, "Fuuuuck!" as Shadow streaks in the door. Dawn's departing energy creates a vacuum Shadow cannot possibly begin to fill.

The old woman's been sitting there for over an hour. She can still feel the warmth along her spine. Dawn is so free with her body, comfortable in it, she is somehow able with her hands to impart something similar to Lillian. *Quite amazing. But what a mouth she has. Foul is what comes out of those full pretty lips. Ah, I hear a pickup truck next door, Dawn's turn for company, of a different sort, I'd guess.*

"Well, I'm off to bed, Shadow. I'll hang my lucky rabbit foot on the bedpost. Sweet dreams."

evening
two blue two large?

The dream, it turns out, is Lillian's, at least in the familiar beginning. She, Lillian, fleet, small, and low to the cold dark ground, agile as all get-out, walking, running, stretching. Now, she, Shadow, cannot stop stretching, forcing her muscles apart, together, rhythmically, sometimes in tandem, making herself long or tall. What absurd joy there is in the nighttime body, regardless of which body Lillian is inhabiting.

In this feline body, curiosity takes the place of insecurity, fear diminishes to caution. This new, or temporarily and nocturnally reborn Lillian sniffs and pads her way along the tiny paths throughout the garden and yard. Barriers that would deter the human Lillian reveal possible passageways until they are not barriers at all. Over. Under. Through. Climbing a tree, she sees not only to the fenced-in yard and house, but farther, into Dawn's unruly, forbidden zone.

There is a porch light on at Dawn's front door, no car in the drive. Lillian, as Shadow-cat, is free to nose around the younger woman's territory—the sweet rankness of her garbage bin, the sour smell of loosely stacked beer cartons, Dawn's enticing foot aroma still clinging to a pair of sneakers near the doormat and flip-flops haphazardly tossed. Harold's old wicker rocker still sits next to the door and by jumping onto it, unbothered by the slight motion she creates, she can peer into Dawn's private domain. Night-eyes make indoor light unnecessary. A payback of sorts for Dawn's earlier perusal. "Pigsty" had not been an exaggeration. Dirty dishes on the counter, half-empty glasses on the small kitchen table next to a computer. Clothing dropped or strewn along a couch. Disorder, in general. Something a cat can appreciate.

Shadow hears the approaching sound of an engine. It's not Dawn's car, but a motorcycle, a big one, manoeuvred by a man big enough to dwarf the woman tucked behind him. By the time it's roared into the double-wide's driveway, Shadow has crouched beneath the rocker, making herself inconspicuous.

Dawn climbs off the bike, removing her helmet while she leans into the driver. The smell of her heavy perfume is mixed with his maleness, his leather, and the hot engine. But despite the coolness of the night, it's the smell of desire that causes Shadow to pay even closer attention. Big Mike, she calls him, and Manly-Man in her sultry phone-voice, a little loud against the sudden quiet of the night. "C'mon, baby," she says, rubbing his shoulder, his neck, while he's slipping off his own helmet and dropping it to ground. "Just do me."

Mike laughs past his small goatee. "Right here?" He slides his hand up under her jacket.

"Fuck, your hands are like ice. Good ice."

"Let's go in."

"Nah." Dawn's hands move to his thighs, his crotch. There is the distinct sound of a heavy belt buckle sliding open. Mike grunts something affirmative.

"Let's go in," he repeats.

"C'mon. Right here, right now. There's no one around."

"What's the point then? Public sex needs an audience. Let's crack a beer, have a toke, get naked and comfortable."

"Sure, fine, but ... " Dawn slides her mouth over his, her hands stroking his neck, his closely shaved head, before guiding one of his relaxed hands toward the heat between her legs. As if a man like Mike needs guidance. He has his own ideas, swinging his leg over the seat, turning smoothly, cupping the cheeks of her ass, startling her briefly with his hard squeeze.

"Got any whisky?" Mike asks, still thinking, perhaps, more about his liquid high, his revving road high, rather than the prospect of sex.

"Mm-hmm. For after ... " She smiles into the night. "If you're good."

"I'm always good."

"We'll see."

"We will." Mike spits halfway across the yard, lifts her over his shoulder, ignoring her caterwauling. "If you're gonna moon the moon, sugar, you really should do it on the quiet. You'll wake the neighbours."

"Neighbour, ya big shithead." She drops her voice. "One. Old."

He carries Dawn onto the porch, dropping her into the rocker. Mike is in through the unlocked door before Dawn stops cursing, to say, "It's open." Shadow can see him heading for the kitchen, dropping his coat and reaching for the bottle on the table. "Hey!" Dawn calls from the porch rocker, then louder, "Hey!" She stumbles through the door after the manly man.

Shadow creeps back to the window, wondering what indignant sex looks like. There is more to this than meets the eye. Even a cat's eye. Even the eyes of a cat with nine lives. The sounds emanating from the far bedroom aren't that hard to decipher—somewhere between pleasure and pain without the smell of fear.

Shadow turns tail for home, Lillian's home. She takes down a good-sized rabbit near a cedar fencepost with barely an effort, snapping its neck but purposefully leaving it intact. Triumphant, somewhat satisfied, she lugs the body home, drops it on the doormat and lets out a small howl of her own. But there is no one to hear it.

Lillian awakens in her warm bed, her delicious bed. No, wait. Her suddenly too warm daylit bed with her hand between her too warm legs. A taste of blood on her tongue. Neither is unpleasant.

black   red   night   bed   pleasure   pain   rabbit   dead

What the hell, thinks Lillian, feeling better by the minute. A dream. A puzzle. Lillian remains in bed, mulling over the dream, night-thoughts, body awareness. The usual stiffness in her joints and the accompanying pain are noticeably diminished. There are times, even now, when anything feels possible. There are times when possibility demands purpose. And action.

Kim Clark

Shadow Lillian Shadow

Dream becomes reality. The rabbit's perfect body, tan and white, lies on the mat outside the door. It is not something to be feared but instead incites a hunger for life in Lillian. Two feet, two talismans should be more powerful. Even three, although the left is the lucky one. A dinner of fresh meat couldn't hurt either. Strength for this ravenous body. *First things first*—to bring the rabbit in and make sure Shadow stays out. Bend. Stoop. Lift. Movement. *There.* Almost easy.

The trailer is quiet, but Lillian spots a motorcycle in the driveway. She carries the limp body into the kitchen, wrapping it loosely in a black garbage bag, and places it on the table. The door is locked, the drapes left closed. Outdoors would be sensible for cleaning game, but indoors is the only place for privacy. She feels unusual. Hesitation has momentarily flown the coop.

The small bathroom mirror reflects Lillian's face, this morning with clear eyes and, if not exactly a smile, a relaxed mouth, a mouth not pinched with pain. She brushes her grey hair back, lifts her chin, runs her hand across her throat, stands as tall as her petite frame allows. Almost as tall as the faint shadow of Dawn. More like a double exposure reflected in the mirror. Lillian is neither surprised nor curious. If she squints, she can make Dawn disappear. There is something to be said for dreaming, if that's what it is. A long bath later, perhaps with a sprinkle of lavender, would be a lovely treat. And why not? Balm after butchery.

morning
one green   one-half red

    Now, deal with Judy. There's no time to waste. Dial. No answer. *Excellent. A message will be easier.* "Hello, Judy. It's Lillian. I'm sorry.

I won't be needing you for a while. My pension won't allow it. And, well, I'm feeling quite well. Perhaps, after the summer ... Thank-you. Goodbye." *Judy may call back but it's highly unlikely. Her nose will be out of joint.*

Lillian adds a few raisins to her small portion of oatmeal, savours it. The dishes are a breeze and the old sharpening stone is still at the back of the cutlery drawer. The anticipation of working on the rabbit, harvesting more luck, is almost sweet enough to bring a song to her lips. She oils the stone and sharpens the familiar knife, laying it on the table beside the black plastic parcel, an old newspaper and Dawn's tattered book. Harold's book. Oh, she must stay on track here. Lillian has an immediate purpose. And a goal. No TV. No blue dots. No red black cards.

The book has step-by-step instructions and drawings. It seems straightforward, but Lillian soon realizes she has overlooked an important step. Slipping a bibbed apron on, she unwraps the body, admires the fur, the small face, the near-closed eyelids, the slack-muscled legs, feet, and claws, then carries it to the sink. A small tick remains attached just behind the right ear. Dangling the body by the delicate neck, Lillian squeezes the belly, pushing down toward the hips with her thumb, releasing a small amount of urine into the drain. If she was Shadow, cooking preparation would be unnecessary. Raw and bloody would suffice. But Lillian would like to enjoy a cooked meal. One roasted in the oven with rosemary— to stimulate the memory and possibility of the dream, to ward off nightmares, to offer the rabbit a fragrant token of appreciation. It won't hurt to cover the slight but inevitable smell of borax and decay either.

Back at the table, bag open, newspaper spread, she severs the hind feet first, tosses the right one into the garbage bag, reconsiders. She sets both aside, grasps the loose pouch of furred skin over the centre of the ribs, slicing neatly through it, cutting it back where necessary. The rabbit's belly mustn't be punctured. The skin is pulled back, side to side, and rolled up toward the head like a pullover. Lillian saws through the neck, drops the head into the bag. Then does the same with the front socks, allowing the skin to be pulled up over the body and down over the tail, not so easy, and the back stumps. The plastic and newspaper catch what blood there is.

A clean slit down the belly to the genitals makes it quite easy to scoop the guts into the bag. The liver has a little yellow fat along it, apparently a healthy thing. Following the final directions, she pushes her finger through the anus from the inside out, and removes the genitals. The lungs are cleaned out, the neck pushed out.

Lillian washes and examines the meat under running water for telltale bits, then puts it into a roasting pan with water, setting it in the fridge. It's supposed to soak overnight, but a few hours will have to do. The hide is scraped fairly clean, washed, squeezed, and put in a Tupperware container in the freezer. She buries the lucky feet in her borax container, then takes the remains out to the alders and dumps the bag into a natural indentation in the ground. Shadow will make quick work of the mess. The newspaper, even the plastic bag, is shoved into the burning barrel and lit. It only takes moments. The walking stick has become more of an impediment than a help. She thinks back to her dream, the free and easy movement as she carries the stick back to the house, stooping to pick a few small branches of rosemary.

Lillian cleans meticulously, pours a bath, settles in. Her mind is not on the events of the morning, but on things to come, or at least, things that need to be done. Dealing with the pelt, for example.

I'll have to make the trip into town. No Judy to pick up groceries for me. And that's just fine. I can do this myself. Must do it myself. It'll be good to drive. Haven't done it for a while. Slow and cautious. Don't hurry. There will be people to deal with, but the liquor store and grocery are side

Solitaire

by side. The way I feel today should make it easy. I'll rest if I need to when I get back. Play a few games after a rosemary dinner. The thought makes my mouth water. Preserving the skin, tanning, can be done tomorrow. A few days for the boraxed feet to cure. And then what? More dreaming? Perhaps, but there are no directions, no helpful list. At least, not yet. Something will show me. Shadow?

alum   pickling salt (to prevent black)   sherry   hair dye (red)

The car, sporting a thick coat of alder pollen, starts up just fine. Lillian warms it up for several minutes. A light drizzle has begun, sending rivulets of powdery chartreuse down the windshield while intensifying the excess of green shoots and budding leaves all 'round. The clumps of tiger lily against the house are pushing up, and the maidenhair fern too, its corm still spiky from neglect. Green is not the dominant colour over in Dawn's yard.

Out on the road, a little slick from the rain, Lillian drives carefully. It's a good feeling to have control and keep it. She makes her way down the cedar-lined hill, past the post office, slowing by the Cedar Arms—Dawn's place of employment—as though it was something curious and new. The parking lot is nearly empty, just waiting for the after-work crews, the gaggle of young folks, the darkness outside that will draw drinkers and talkers and partiers to its warm light.

The Cedar Grocery, monopolized by women and small children at this time of day, takes longer than she had expected. Not because of her slow walking. She's moving more easily now. Still, it takes time to find the items she needs while avoiding the odd familiar face. And the "pleasantries." *How are you, dear? Ready for spring? Where's Judy Mitchell today? I thought she shopped for you. Do you need a hand, Ma'am?* Thankfully, most shoppers go on about their business. She finds the hair dye easily. Apricot Blush.

There is no one in the tiny liquor store but a middle-aged man stacking cases of beer. He directs her to the sherries and parks himself behind the till. She settles on Harveys Bristol Cream, gets a chuckle out of the name, takes the bottle up to the counter to pay. She hesitates, then asks him for two more bottles, which he retrieves, takes her money, and carries them out to her car.

She is done, and just in the nick of time. There is pastel Judy with an empty shopping cart. *Damn small towns!*

Home is waiting. By the time Lillian makes the two trips from car to house, she is physically tired but pleased with herself as though she'd gotten away with something. Ever so small but something nonetheless.

She reads the directions for the hair dye but divides the recipe in half—something to be said for those specifics, another new task. Another challenge. The result, after applying the colour for half the recommended time, shampoo, rinse, and towel dry, is not dramatic. Simply a brighter frame around her face. It would do fine. For now. Lillian digs out an old blow-dryer. The heat seems to pull out not only the fresh new colour but a little wave. Better.

The rosemaried rabbit goes into the oven. The timer is set. Potatoes peeled. Tomatoes sliced before the old achiness sets in. *Sit, Lillian,* she thinks.

red   black red   black red   black

Ah, the mindless but orderly cards. Kings and queens. Jacks ... or knaves. A much better name. I'd like a new name. To go with the slightly improved me. Lillian is so, well, old-fashioned. An old name for an old woman, and I am sick of both, sick of myself, the way I have been. One thing at a time.

The TV must stay on for drying out the rabbit feet. I turn up the volume just a little, even for the six o'clock news. Economy. Bail-out. Environment. Olympics. Security. Shutdowns. Homeless. Gangs. Guns. Just as well I can only hear bits and pieces. Fashion models in New York start a riot. Nonsense. Another human foot found on a beach too close to home. That is enough. Picture, no sound. Maybe the radio will be better. Some music with dinner. The meat is sizzling in the oven, giving off a delectable aroma. I can't wait. Time to put the potatoes on. I may just mash them for a treat. And there will be plenty of both to warm up tomorrow. Less work then, although I'm kind of enjoying my day. Busy purpose. New and old. Sweet and bitter. In and out and round-about. What a day, indeed. A sprig of this rosemary under my pillow might just improve my night.

Lillian relishes every bite of her meal—the succulent meat tastier than any chicken with its pungent near-piney rosemary, the creamy heavily buttered potatoes, the bright tart tomato slices. Each sip of sherry is a sweet mouthful of summer, taunting the increasing wind and rain against the window. Shadow is allowed a few tidbits from the dinner plate. Usually a no-no, but things in general—in Lillian's small world at least—seem due for some relaxation therapy, both physical and mental. A change of rules. Maybe even toss a few rules out. Choices. Opportunities. Joy. And luck. She admits, accepts these are part of what it's about, being alive.

Leaning back in her chair with Shadow in her lap, Lillian feels sated. She nods off, snaps awake with a word on her tongue. *Lily! Now that is a name to live up to.*

The radio provides background noise, then suddenly, "One rabbit does not make a summer, neither does one fine day." Good grief. Had she heard that right? It rings a bell, but its connection to this day is bizarre. A prophecy? A clue? It simply can't be. It is Lillian, not Lily, who lurches out of the chair, ignoring Shadow and the sherry bottle, and cranks the radio dial to Off. But it is Lily who laughs and says to herself, "Maybe the medium *is* the message."

Lillian leaves the dishes, bypassing the cards except for a quick flip of the deck. Red, red, nothing but red. She is reminded of something learned decades earlier—that red (ship-wise) means port and left, while green means starboard and right. Short words mean left. Longer words mean right. The word green is equal in length to the word black. Maybe she shouldn't have saved the right hind foot? Would there be a problem? A backlash of magic? The voice in Lillian's head is definitely a Lily voice. A strong new voice, persistent but not yet to be trusted. The three of hearts slips to the floor. Everything seems a sign.

evening
one-half blue   one large?

The coastal rain is relentless for more than a week. Water drips constantly from overflowing gutters. It makes for delicious slumber. A cleansing dreamless lullaby. The lack of dreams is disappointing. Perhaps Lillian has overshot her goal. Dawn is absent, too, for the most part, only appearing late one morning, dashing in and out of the trailer, leaving the car motor running. Even Shadow is hesitant to take on the wetness, sleeping anywhere and everywhere that is warm, dry, and inconspicuous.

    She rests through the nights but during the lengthening days, there are preparations to be made and an unusual appetite to be satisfied. Lists and tasks. She feels stronger. There is little pain and the redness surrounding her joints is fading. She flexes her near-nimble fingers, turns up the desk light. The rabbit feet are removed from the borax, brushed, rubbed, and palmed. Three charms. She dabs a bit of glue over the dried flesh and binds the hewn ends with embroidery thread, red for the two left feet, black for the solo right foot, and braids the ends into small loops. The feet look rather splendid. Not just ornamental, but powerful. Powerful enough to do Lillian some good hidden away in a deep pocket while remaining accessible. But perhaps not strong enough to complete the task still forming in her mind.

    Each day Lillian rubs Nivea cream into her skin. Each day she makes a Lily-improvement, tasks that had been not only frivolous but impossible with gnarled, uncooperative hands. On the second day Lillian manicures her nails. On the third, she plucks her eyebrows, experiments with brown pencil. On the fourth, she re-dyes her hair with the remaining Apricot Blush. Much better this time. A couple of decades better, if she does say so herself.

The clouds finally drift to the north, exposing a feverish morning sun. It is an unbelievable May day. Mist rises from every leaf, branch, and surface, and especially from Dawn's roof. Except for the fresh clean air, it's thick enough to be smoke. With a souped-up black pickup parked just behind Dawn's car, there is likely to be some burning passion under that roof. Shadow exits into the vaporous garden eager for something.

The hands of the clock move slowly through the day.

morning
one-half green   one-half red

The cards now give Lillian an excuse to remain at the window. A plaid-shirted man with a stubbly face is in and out of the truck several times, even swatting at Shadow sitting on the glinting hood. The cat is undeterred. Then Dawn and another woman, hard-pretty, blondish, smoke on her porch. The blonde flicks her hair, drapes her arm casually across Dawn's back, tucks her hand into Dawn's back pocket, laughing. There is a kiss. A kiss that lingers beyond friendship. Music pours from her neighbour's open door, but Lillian detects a tuneful melody within the music. Or her aural taste is shifting. *Oral. Aural.* A Lily-esque puzzle of words. Nothing would surprise Lillian today. Despite the stirrings of jealousy, it is the suit of hearts that dominates.

red   left   heart   red   left   heart

Shadow Lily Shadow

As the day slips away into darkness, Lillian prepares for bed. She tucks fresh rosemary under her pillow, hangs the embellished feet on a small nail at the head of her bed—a small nail in the wall closest to Dawn, as though her energy could be tapped. Shadow sleeps at the foot of the bed, taking advantage of Lillian's relaxed rules.

Lillian is restless, staring into darkness, alert to every sound. The chirrup of frogs, a moth fluttering at the window, Shadow's breathing, the beat of her own heart in battle with the twangy music from next door. Then, finally, she slips into dreaming.

In this dream she makes directly for Dawn's, within the body of Shadow, fleet and agile, and in a Lily state of mind. No hesitation, everything acute. Hard-edged moon. Small splinters breaking through the moss on the worn cedar fencing. A harsh patch of light from the too-bright porch light. Lily leaps to the railing, watches Dawn & Company through the open window, slugging back beers around the kitchen table, sniffing lines of powder from an ornate mirror, a tightly rolled bill to the nostril. Lily holds back, thinks better of it, takes a step past fluttering curtains. She is in—past crusty pizza boxes and the sour of dirty dishes. Slipping under the table amidst all those feet gives her protection and proximity. Between Dawn's painted toes and the runners and leather boots of the others is a little piece of heaven. Above the table, the voices are disjointed but urgent.

"You can't stash it here. I can't take a chance on more trouble. Been there, done that." Lily likes the sound of "trouble" from Dawn's lips. She observes Dawn's feet, not the cleanest, but still attractive. Rosy. Flexible. Lily suppresses the desire to taste. The left foot holds the power and information—the big toe nondescript, but the adjacent toe is as long as those of the Egyptian dynasties, or even Hawaiian. The middle toe is the one that intrigues Lily. Slightly bent at the last joint, it indicates a natural ability to deceive. There is a small bluish dot between the joint and nail. *Perfect. Purrfect.* Lily licks her lips.

The blonde remains speechless, fidgeting with the seam of her jeans while the guy shuffles his boots around. "Well, any suggestions, Houston?"

Houston stops fidgeting. "I dunno, baby."

"Dawn, c'mon. I got a lot of heat around my place. You know I'll pay. Before and after, same as before."

"Not here, Pete," says Dawn.

"Just half a dozen times. That's it."

"Wait a minute. What about Lillian's. She'll never know."

"I don't know no Lillian."

"The old boot next door. I've got an in. Like to surprise her. Don't think she'll be around long anyway. She's fucking ancient."

"Thinkin 'bout scorin' yourself a little more property, Miss Dawn?"

Dawn doesn't answer, but gives him a hard bare-footed shove above one of those boots. *Ooh.*

Lily has to skitter out of the way.

He grunts. "She's not nosy or nothing?"

"One of those private types. Keeps to herself. I'll figure it out. How soon?"

"A week, maybe. I'll let you know."

Houston gives Dawn a loose caress over her bare thigh and drawls, "Cool. Done deal. Pass the mirror, hon."

Lily knows, just as Lillian did, there is more to Dawn than meets the eye. The talkers shift gears, rev up the mood, wander from the kitchen to the bathroom, to the stereo, to the fridge for more cold brews. Pete lights the stove-top element, waits for red heat, calls the girls over for a little hot-knife hit. Aromatic smoke.

They tilt between anxiety and euphoria, never quite together like pinballs at odds in a game of overindulgence. The trio are oblivious. And conveniently on their way to incoherence.

Dawn sings along to the music periodically. "Give me your heart" and "Got a black magic woman." Lily takes it all in. And waits.

Pete finally passes out on the couch, leaving Dawn and the blonde with her head in her hands, at the table. The stereo runs out of music after "Cat Scratch Fever." Lily takes the opportunity, a plan in her sharp mind, to get Dawn outside. She exits soundlessly through the window, wishing she could accomplish this deed at the height of some passionate moment, Dawn's pupils dilated with lust rather than chemicals, but there is no time. Lily drags three thorny blackberry branches at intervals across the steps of Dawn's front porch. She pushes an empty brown bottle from the railing. Thud. Another two, smashing against the third. Perhaps she has waited too long. But no, she hears movement from within. A mumbled, "What the fuck?!" Lily has already positioned herself on the bottom step when the door is flung open, and there she is, Dawn in all her pissed-off glory, perfectly unsteady on her feet. "Better not be a fuckin' bear out there," she yells. Lily twitches, makes a sound, a high moan, enough to get attention. She's been seen.

Dawn moves closer, takes a step down, catches her ankle on the vicious stem of blackberry. "Christ! Fuck! Owww!" but she doesn't go down, just tips to the side and slowly sits against the post, examining the droplets of blood accumulating on the darkening lines of broken skin. She tries to brush them away. Dawn glances back to the cat. Lily flutters her eyes, makes a pathetic movement. Dawn is immobile for a few seconds. "Hey, Kitty, you alive?" A small mew. It's when Dawn leans in closer to get a better look that Lily crawls just out of reach, and Dawn loses her balance, falls indelicately from the steps. Expletives follow. The tumble is nothing serious, but enough to be remembered the following morning. She rolls onto her back sloppily. Lily waits. "Houston!" Dawn finally calls, but with diminished energy. "Pete! Houston! Hey, you shitheads!" Dawn mumbles something and closes her eyes, her breathing slows.

Even the vulnerable soles of her feet are exposed. *Soles, souls,* thinks Lily. She feels more like a Cheshire than a tortoiseshell. Lily makes one precise slash with her claws, eliciting a jerk and moan from Dawn. Nothing more. Beautiful red lines emerge across the two longest toes of the left foot, knuckle to tip.

She worries the narrow wound on the middle toe with her harsh tongue, insistent, relentless, nibbling away at morsels of flesh to expose muscle, tendon, and finally the prize—bone. Small and vital. Extrication is difficult. Delicate work. Disengaging the joint takes one precise snap of the jaw. A pull with her teeth, a push with her paws, and it is out. Using her nose and tongue, she pushes the skin at the sides of the wound back to near touching. Excellent. She carries the bone carefully in her teeth, making her way back home. She perches on the cedar fence cleaning the bone, cleaning herself, imagining Dawn waking, wandering slowly into the trailer, confused in her scratched, bloody state. Maybe curling into the arms of that Pete-guy on the couch. Maybe finding Houston in her unkempt bed. Her foot throbbing. Tomorrow the infection will set in.

Kim Clark

Lily   Shadow   Lily

It is Lily who awakens in Lillian's bed, a high full sun through the curtains, Shadow curled by her knees, spent, tongue lolling. Energy radiates through the woman from her clenched fist. *The bone! Plans need to be made. To hell with cards, with meds, with patient old ideas.*

It takes the next three days to dry out the bone after scrubbing and borax. Three days to maintain an outer semblance of public Lillian. Later there will be withdrawals at the bank as Lillian, a trip out past Cedar and over the bridge. A couple of big malls across Nanaimo would supply her with what she needed: a stockpile of groceries, trendy magazines guiding the naïve through a plethora of beauty products, cosmetics, something new to wear. A musky perfume. Then alternately, as a newer younger model, Lily, opening a new account at a bank across town. Shopping for clothing. Getting a pedicure with red polish. Maybe even those acrylics for her fingertips.

Lily is not idly waiting for the curing bone. She checks the mirror often. Her skin is firmer, rosier, healthy. Her hair thickening nicely. Her lips less pinched. Her whole body is shifting, the back straightening, breasts filling out with a perky lift. Examining her feet and hands, there are no longer apparent bulges or gnarls. They are not unpretty. All the while she is thinking, planning, and by the second day, with no sign of Dawn, she is worrying. The lights next door remain on late into the night. Her car has not moved. There has been no activity at all, which could be good or very, very bad. Lily cannot sleep. She watches TV, unbothered by commercials, reality shows, late-night comedians, even sitcoms. She needs to learn about the zippy young culture, have a few names and events to drop here and there. She checks the window often for signs of trouble. And finally sees Dawn, on day three, hobbling out to her car, a grimace on her face. She definitely looks alive, although taking slow, very cautious steps, favouring her left leg. When Dawn leaves, Lily, masquerading as Lillian, putters about the garden, staying close to the cedar fence in wait. She has to see for herself. She deadheads spent blooms of geranium, rose, marguerite to draw out the new growth, tugs dandelion and thistle, sees the first unfurled petals of tiger lily despite the voracious nibbling of rabbits. Minutes slip into an hour. Then another. Crowns of bleeding heart are divided with a sharp-edged shovel. The sun is high and hot, making the sweater unbearable. Lily is hungry, thirsty, impatient with waiting. Dawn doesn't disappoint. She pulls into her driveway, yanks a pair of crutches from the back seat, and hobbles toward her front porch, keeping the bandaged foot well off the ground. It's Lily's turn to force a conversation. She moves closer to the low fence. She's wearing a garden hat, sunglasses, the old sweater once again, with the walking stick for good measure.

"Goodness, Dawn, what have you done to yourself?" Lily's voice has the desired effect.

"Christ, Lillian!" Dawn nearly jumps out of her skin. The younger woman seems oblivious to the changes in Lily. Dawn's left calf is red, ripe with thick dark scratches, and puffy above the wrapped bandage. She looks weary and faded beneath a feverish slick. "Yeah, I did a number on my foot. I dunno what happened. I fell, I guess, got buggered up in the blackberries." She turns awkwardly away. "Gotta go."

Lily's not done. "Must have been a nasty accident. You really don't look well."

"Yeah, tell me about it. I feel like crap. And now it's infected. Antibiotics," she says, holding out her hand, also bandaged. "IV every day for a week ... Yeah, right. How'm I gonna work? Fuck. I can't hardly walk, never mind get into a pair of shoes. I really gotta go before I pass out or something." Dawn curses under her breath as she heads for the porch.

"Well, let me know if you need anything. I'm just next door." The words disperse into the heat. Back to business, Lily thinks as she peels off her sweater and strides up the steps and into the coolness of home. Satisfied there is no suspicion or memory of the event, she calls Shadow, offers a treat and a pat, and says, "It's alright. It's all right."

On the third day, when she is completely satisfied with the drying process, Lily considers a small surgery on herself, placing the bone beneath her own skin. Body modification, they call it. But her body could reject it no matter how much her soul wanted its power. Instead, she cleans the small bone for the final time, polishes it, works a darning needle through the tiny bulbous end, patiently rotating the needle between her fingers as though the friction might spark a miniature fire. Lily knows the fire is within. A hot passion. Red embroidery thread is fed through the hole, wrapped meticulously around the top end. A beautiful pale pendant to drop between her breasts and wear next to her heart.

That night, another dream. Shadow travels farther afield, down to the Cedar Arms. It's not yet midnight. She has no trouble gaining entry. The door is open.

The interior is cozy but worn, dimly lit. The walls are arrayed with new beer posters and yellowing local photos, but it's the mounted elk head above the bar that is so mesmerizing. The art of taxidermy hidden away in the neighbourhood pub. And there is more. A stuffed otter on the east wall, a lynx on the west. Shadow shivers but carries on with reconnaissance.

The owner isn't hard to pick out, a dark wiry Irishman behind the bar in casual conversation—post-hockey-season parley over pints of beer—opposite a couple of guys on the lean, work boots on the rail. A few people are clustered in the back room. She noses around the place, scopes out the tables, booths, the hallway leading to washrooms, and especially the kitchen—brightly lit but empty at this time of night. She pays attention to mannerisms, attitudes, scattered small talk.

A middle-aged man in a black T-shirt rests his paunch against the bar, slurry but not unattractive. His buddy is forgettable. The rear booth houses a slinky sandalled brunette sporting an overdose of eye makeup and unkempt toenails. She's with a couple of hefty biker-boys and an older fellow, a balding beanpole with a contemptuous voice, a frequent harsh laugh. Highballs on the table. A winsome young couple, sporty and tanned, smooch over bottles of tropical something-or-other at the incongruous techno-jukebox. Shadow catches threads of lyric as the music switches from rock—"I could use somebody" to country—"Diggin' up bones," then back again.

It's enough for now. Time to exit before closing time. An accidental overnight lock-up could get dicey. As she heads for the door, a twitter from the sporty smoocher-girl cuts through the near-silent gap between songs. "Hey, look! Here, Kitty. Kitty, Kitty! Grab him, babe. I just love cats." The boyfriend shrugs, nonplussed, but steps toward the feline, stooping. Shadow hisses and arches, then hightails it out into the sure cover of night. "Aw, you scared it ... " The girl's voice fades away.

On the fourth day Dawn responds to Lily's knock with a dull expletive. "What? Yeah, come on in. That you, Houston? Pete?" Then nothing.

"It's me. Lillian." She pushes open the door, stands there stooped in her gardening get-up, covered for the most part. "I brought you some soup. It's still hot. Goodness, you're not yourself."

"No, I'm not. Not at all," Dawn says from her curled position on the couch. "Feel about a hundred years old with a temperature to match." She's surrounded by a litter of half-empty cups, bottles, used tissues. The TV is droning. "I was sleeping."

Lily makes a space on the coffee table for the soup. "You've lost weight. Not eating?" Indeed, Dawn's face is almost gaunt. She grunts noncommittally, sits up, dropping the blanket from her shoulders, props her foot on the table, nearly spilling the soup. The tattoos are still there but lackluster, muted.

"The foot's a little better. The rest of me feels like shit."

"I won't stay. Go back to sleep."

"Yeah, good plan."

"Goodbye, Dawn."

Dawn yawns, already settling back into her nest, a broken diminishing bird. "Thanks, eh."

Lily closes the door behind her.

Lily Lily Lily

Day five. Lily is showered, refreshed, blow-dried, light makeup applied. Her new hair extensions drift down her bare back. Maybe a place for a tattoo. Down low. She slips into a new pair of jeans, hip-hugging snug, and a rich red tank top, not too revealing. Large gold hoops for her newly pierced earlobes and a heavily buckled black leather belt spiff things up enough. Looking over her selection of new shoes, she chooses black heels, not stilettos but sexy.

She makes an afternoon foray into the quiet pub, chats with the owner, Richard, a server, Beth, otherwise keeping to herself. She's brought a newspaper to send out the message Occupied. What Lily would like is a glass of sherry. Not likely to find anything decent here. What she orders is wine, a Shiraz, peppy red. The menu is surprisingly lengthy. The daily special will do—a Reuben sandwich with salad.

"Do you know of any work around here, Richard?" Lily asks as she pays her tab, passing a bill with her immaculate fingers. He's pleased, she can tell, that she remembers his name and says it with an open smile.

"You looking?"

"Oh, yeah. Not much out there."

Richard hesitates. A good sign. "Uh, not really."

"Too bad. You've got a real nice place here."

Lily turns to go, pushing her new wallet into her flashy oversized bag, prolonging the moment.

"Hey, why don't you check back tomorrow? Staff's a bit up in the air. What's your name, by the way?"

"Lily." She nods thanks, and makes her way back out into the sunlight with a special swing to her hips, aware of the eyes on her.

Day seven, a Friday. Lily pulls into the jam-packed parking

lot of the Cedar Arms. It's late afternoon, warm and promising. She's dressed down a bit, to a tight black T-shirt, its deep V exposing glimpses of her amulet, and flats. She has polished herself into newness. Fingering the rabbits' feet in her pocket, she slides into a vacant booth just left of the mounted lynx, newspaper in hand, making eye contact with Richard pouring frantically behind the bar.

It's loud, mostly men at week's end, ready to let loose. Dust and sweat mingle with the smell of beer, pizza, fish and chips. Richard hustles over after collecting a tray of empties.

"What can I get for you today?"

"That Shiraz, I guess."

"Menu?"

"No thanks. Already eaten. Just the wine."

He heads off through the tables and customers, returns moments later without the wine, asking, "You got any experience, Lila?"

"It's Lily. Experience?"

"Lily. Sorry. Yeah, waitressing, serving drinks, pouring beer?"

"As a matter of fact, I do have experience ... waiting. Just not behind the bar."

"You got plans for the night?"

"Plans?"

"Look. I need a hand. Beth's off sick and Dawn, uh, the other server, is giving me the runaround. Some fake-ass excuse again."

Lily hesitates, just long enough. "You're on."

Richard is taken aback by the quick acceptance. He pauses, glancing around the crowded bar. "Okay. Follow me, Lily. We'll work out the formalities later, just talk it through on the run. See how things go."

The night flies. There are mistakes, singles rather than doubles, Lucky instead of Miller, three broken glasses, spillage. But Lily has a way of making even the whiners smile. The guys, at least. Other than a slight scuffle at the pool table, the mood stays high. These folks are serious about their weekend exuberance.

Lily is serious, too, behind the smile, the hip-swing, the hair-toss. People skills. Richard has been too busy to crack more than a couple of jokes. He seems impressed with her calmness under pressure, even without knowledge of the regulars' idiosyncrasies. No ice. Lime on the side. Beer in a sleeve. Coke for the designated driver in a pint glass. Etcetera. Etcetera. The patrons gobble unusual food—fried bread, Greek dip, wraps instead of sandwiches.

It takes Lily a couple of forty-hour weeks, only the night shifts, to inure herself. Beth is the permanent day-girl who doesn't hang around after her shift and Lily doesn't arrive early. The night-cook is a companionable man who rarely throws a plate. The place thrives on small talk: the hot summer expected ahead, plummeting real estate prices, a bust on River Road, mill jobs disappearing, again. Food, drink, and that's about it. And well, Dawn's name comes up, the first week or so. *She got sick or something.* Lily hears, plays dumb. *Just hasn't shown up.* "Really," she comments, heart quickening.

It's not hard to stay under the radar. Lily sticks to her story. When asked, she's from Alberta, staying with friends near the hospital downtown. No she has no relatives on the coast. Yes, she's thinking of looking for a place out here in Cedar. "Know of anything?" she asks, but she knows she's fine where she is, for now. She wants to keep Lillian's old place as a sanctuary, free from company, prying eyes and wagging tongues. A few of the guys give her the come-on, regardless of age or marital status. Hard to tell sometimes. Blue collars seldom wear rings. A "compo" issue, they say, when called out on it. She doesn't think Workers' Compensation has anything to do with it.

The casual constant touching is unnerving. A pat on the arm, a touch to the shoulder, the brush of a denim thigh or silky back. All those bodies filtering through the dim light makes for a sloppy social dance that becomes an exquisite fascination. Lily shows no response, but her blood pulses electric. She memorizes even the irrelevant names attached to the tabs they run. But no one body draws her, brings her desire to the surface. Night after night, it is the same. Lily will have to change up the game, focus, pay more attention. The novelty of self-appreciation is wearing off, and the previous mortification of the virginal state of her body has recovered from the sacrificial stab and pressure of none other than Harold's rabbit-crested walking stick. The symbolism, at the time, had not been lost on Lily—proliferation and rebirth.

Lily must not let herself slide back. The cards are dead. The only red-black she needs are in her apparel, alternating days. She pores over magazines through the night, scoring high on the enclosed "hottie" quizzes, and watches late-night TV—sources of social education. Men are attracted to red more than blue. Artificial pheromones can illicit an internal sexual response. The smell of cinnamon buns or pumpkin pie or lavender has been proven to boost male erections and attractions in general. The Cedar Arms is a seductive and odorous battlefield.

There are difficulties. Shadow is restless in her absence, arriving over the fence with a mouse or dark murky feathers, long after Lily gets home. Dawn's condition is a potential problem.

Another Friday——a "red" night. Lily recognizes Houston, the wispy blonde from Dawn's. She takes her beer order, nonchalantly asking if she'd like menus, plural.

Houston is quiet, nervous. "Nah. Just me. No tab. I'll pay cash." She appears to actually have a thought as well as a wallet stuffed with money. "How long you worked here?"

"Just started. I'm the newbie."

"Hmm. You never met Dawn then?"

"She hasn't been here. I heard she was sick."

"Yah, she's sick alright. Bad.Some flesh-eating disease or

something. She's in the hospital here, but they're talking about sending her down to Victoria."

Lily heads over to the far tables, mentally filing the information. It's the knife she notices first, being slid beneath the table. It's not hefty, but the open blade catches her eye.

"You can't have that in here." Lily waits, trying to gauge the stranger, the situation. "It's considered a weapon. In a public house." The eyes, those eyes, that look up at her are a bright blue, shining, intelligent, smoking hot. Wavy brown hair, a sensuous mouth, a long lean body folded into the booth, in work duds—jeans and a grey wool shirt. A startling pair of oversized workboots—a scruffy tear in the left toe revealing steel. Deliciously young, even younger than Dawn, smelling woody and subtly frisky.

"Geez, sorry. I was just finishing something up." Shy, maybe. Embarrassed grin but direct gaze.

Lily notices a small dusting of shavings on the tabletop, peers over the table, inhaling his masculinity in the process. His long fingers are holding a tiny wooden shape.

"What do you think?" He holds it up in the palm of his hand.

"Wow. It's a snake. A really beautiful coiled snake. So much detail. But why the wings?"

"It's a serpent," he says, flipping the knife shut and pulling down the neck of his T-shirt to reveal the tip of a tattoo, "like this one."

"Nice. Very nice. I'm impressed, but the knife has to go. I can put it behind the bar for you. What's your name?"

"Hayden." He hands the knife over, slipping the winged figure into his pocket.

"Okay, Hayden. We're good to go. What'll it be?" Lily wants to climb into his pocket after the serpent. But it's a busy night. She is aware of him leaving after a couple of pints, alone.

She, too, goes home alone. She passes a pickup pulling out

of her cedar-lined dead-end roadway. Three possible scenarios: a driver lost, a driver coming from Lillian's—impossible, or a driver coming from Dawn's—just maybe, but Dawn has abandoned the double-wide trailer for the hospital.

Shadow is out by the old garden shed, refusing to come in. Lily is wide awake, pours herself a glass of wine but feels unsettled, wary. Shadow is yowling around. Unusual. Lily dons her faithful sweater, transfers the rabbits' feet and a flashlight to the bulky knitted pocket, thinks of the stranger pocketing his serpent. She steps outside.

There is a clatter. Ah. Shadow is toying with some dead thing amidst faded pots in the shed. That is all. *Or, is it?* The dead thing is not animal. It's the sloughed-off skin of a snake, transparent in the beam of light. A beautiful thing, really. Lily laughs, scoops the snakeskin into her pocket when Shadow loses interest, sniffing at a new prize perhaps. The smell of damp earth is quite strong, as though it's been disturbed. She picks up the shovel, fresh soil halfway to the shoulder of the blade.

An hour later Lily is back in the house. It is the first time she has been truly exhausted in weeks. She sleeps heavily, fearlessly, Shadow at her feet, surrounded by charms.

It takes a couple of weeks. No knife this time. Good boy. Same table. Same stretch of leg. The eyes are more direct, more curious. Lily has studied mannerisms enough to know how much to reveal.

"Hayden."

"You remembered me."

"Absolutely. What can I get for you tonight?"

"Hmm, just a beer, please."

"You're not from around here, are you, Hayden?"

"Nope. Alberta. North of Lethbridge. A little place called Bony River." He leans forward. "What about you? You got a name?"

"Lily." There is definitely attraction. "I'll get that beer."

An hour before the shift's over, he makes a move, leans in as she's counting change. "Let me take you home."

"It's against policy. Y'know."

"You don't strike me as a woman who worries about policies."

"You any good?" Lily knows she's flustered him.

"I'm not some kid just out of high school. Believe me." He looks a little hurt.

"I want to kiss you. Just not here."

Lily knows she can't take him home. Won't take him home, to Lillian's. "Where you staying?"

"Anywhere you like."

"Downtown."

He names a hotel in the old city quarter. "I'll wait for you."

"Not likely. I'll meet you. The hotel lot. Ninety minutes."

"I want to kiss you back."

Lily smiles, runs a fingernail down the back of his hand.

Hayden finishes his beer, saunters out saying, "Have a good night."

Lily knows it will be good. She is hotter than a firecracker.

When she pulls into the hotel parking lot, he's there, sliding his long legs into the passenger side of her car. "Now the kiss."

There's little need to talk. They head inside. Civility in public. Lily likes that. The night then is filled with the ebb and flow of unabashed, unrelenting desire—the stretch and curl of muscles, bodies rhythmically in tandem. What absurd joy in the nighttime body. Aromas. Tastes. Sounds. And laughter. Nothing emotionally complicated. No ridiculous attempts at romance. Simple pleasure. Skin to skin. Dirty sweet.

The pale morning wakes Lily. The red thread of her amulet is wrapped around Hayden's carved serpent on the bedside table. Fitting. The midnight cowboy snores gently beside her. She strokes his beautiful back while breathing him in and slips away out of bed, wanders to the windowless bathroom, flicks the light on, glances in the mirror, feeling rosy. Everywhere. It must show.

The mirror reveals her nakedness, a slight bruise near the right nipple, a flush at the throat. She carries his scent on her body, the palms of her hands, runs them over her flesh and up, up to her face. Lily is there in the mirror. She peers closer. Panic. The flaw is apparent, crow's feet reappearing, the etching of age. A slight tic below the eyebrow. The trickster at work. There is the faint shadow of Dawn behind her. And there farther back, a much taller blur. Multiple exposures. If she squints, she can make them disappear.

She knows she will go home to Lillian's, lay out her collection of charms on the bed. Rabbit's feet for luck and shapeshifting. Rosemary for memory and fending off evil spirits. Dawn's bone for transformation. The snakeskin for renewal. Hayden's serpent for rebirth. And there, leaning in the corner will be Harold's walking stick. The shape and size of the serpent and rabbit inexplicably similar. They could have been carved by the same knife, the same long fingers. Bony River, eh? A trip to Alberta isn't out of the question. That little windfall stashed in the shed could go quite a ways.

Lily is not done with him yet. Composing herself, she approaches the bed. Hayden has turned onto his belly, exposing his rounded buttocks, those muscular thighs. His feet dangle well beyond the foot of the bed, free of sheets, free of anything at all. She cannot resist the sole. She caresses the left, runs her nail slowly down from heel to toe, then her tongue. She sighs. Just one more taste.

Six Degrees of Altered Sensation

~~HHt HHt~~ ll Days of Xmas

On the first day of Xmas I try, I really do, to get into the spirit of the season. I sit down at my desk, push aside the papers, bills, books, and make a list. Slowly, thoughtfully. Words flow along the lined paper. But on reading it over, I realize it's too much to do, to try to do, to even think about doing. Time is of the essence, my mother used to say to make me hurry. I think my essence is telling me I need to let something go, so I cross out ornaments with all their traditional personal baggage and opt to decorate the tree with photos instead. I don't have to look for the photos, either. Those boxes are still stacked at the foot of my bed, a mere six months since the big move. Separation.

> 1. People SHOP
> 2. Xmas dinner SHOP
> 3. Cards
> 4. Tree?
> 5. ~~Ornaments~~ PHOTOS
> 6. Liquor

I'll hit the stores now, and start at the bottom—liquor. I don't want lights this year, I think, as I head out with my list. In fact, if I could afford to be somewhere warm without any Xmas I would "X" it totally from my calendar. And I'm not alone in this. There is a snowballing underground movement to abolish the whole mess. People are actually giving away Xmas heirlooms. Throwing out twenty-year-old cards. Refusing to buy three pounds of butter for shortbread. Even the manager of the liquor store admits out the side of his mouth that he sent the store decorations to the Sally Ann. What spirits!

When I get home, I see I'm too late. My Xmas-diehard neighbour has strung coloured lights along my one-storey roof for me.

Kim Clark

I bite my pride, swallow ingratitude and choke back my tongue. Why would someone do that? Yeah, I know why. It's the cane and the need for the cane and the fact that I can't bend over to pick up the newspaper without losing my visual connection and landing on my ass. In my case, it's called MS. It rhymes with depress, which is too bizarre for state-of-the-art peace of mind. It's the fact that I'm a new neighbour and I live alone. It's the assumption I must need help and want cheering up, and in fact, I just want to rip down the lights and shove them up someone's ass. But it's kind of slippery out there and downright dangerous. Right. As soon as I manage to get my coat and hat and scarf and mitts off, I walk over to the table and cross Cards off the list. It's too late anyway. Be realistic. My address book has so many scratch-outs it's almost impossible to navigate. Harder than the narrow front porch where the newspaper lands every morning.

    1. *People SHOP*
    2. *Xmas dinner SHOP*
    3. ~~*Cards*~~
    4. *Tree?*
    5. ~~*Ornaments*~~ *PHOTOS*
    6. *Liquor*

I'm still not a total humbug. There is one seasonal tradition I do have serious respect for, and one I am counting on to balance the universe. It involves this great rush of wind that blows down from the north the very first night the lights are strung and lit so that they swing and dip, losing their plastic grasp of the gutter. They clatter and burst against the siding, vinyl or otherwise, with every gust, and coloured shards of glass rain down through leafless branches. Random gaps of shadow hide barren sockets in need of pliers-extrication. Somebody pretty important is pissed off, indignant, embarrassed with our showy-needy-want instead of just need, and I don't mean that in a sexual way. There is always a neighbourly flurry of ladder activity the day after. Panic over broken pattern.

On the second day of Xmas, I notice a voice message on my cell phone. Unknown name. Unknown number. I listen to the message three times. It's always the same.

"Hey, Marvin. It's me, man. You shouldn't come home for a while. I'll explain later. When I phone you back." But I don't know any Marvin.

I wonder how good things will be for him in a day, a week. "Me-man" never calls back. I hope next time he dialled the right number, for chrissake. Merry Xmas, Marvin. Brings to mind my trip to the undecorated liquor store. The least I can do for Marvin is raise my glass and wish him well. I'll raise my glass to Chuck Palahniuk, too. His book, *Choke*, is the closest I can come to spiritual reading this holiday season. I have crossed the anti-Christmas line. I have also crossed Tree off my list. Environmentally unfriendly any way you look at it. And the photos can stay in the box. Considering my rate of consumption, I put liquor back on the list.

1. People SHOP
2. Xmas dinner SHOP
3. ~~Cards~~
4. ~~Tree~~
5. ~~Ornaments~~ PHOTOS
~~6. liquor~~
& 7. LIQUOR

On the third day of Xmas, I escape a hangover by the skin of my teeth, but Noel, my brother in the Interior, calls and I reach for the ibuprofen when I see his number on the call display. Well, it seems his belligerent girlfriend used his sweet '69 Mustang to lay a lickin' on the oak doors of the pub in the Nicola River Hotel. Noel says she tried to justify it by saying the pub won't allow male strippers or Salvation Army Santas. Or maybe it's the other way around: female Santas or Salvation Army strippers. They might both make more money, I think to myself. One of the cops out on the call fell on the ice and broke his coccyx. Then "someone" threw a piece of the door into the pub's fireplace to hold off the minus-twenty wind whistling through the new "wind-ow" in the door. Things got ugly after that. Oh, Noel. They won't make it down to the coast for the big day.

On the fourth day of Xmas, the news channel tells me that fruitcake, like the one I considered sending to my cousin in Yemen, is the same density as plastic explosives, causing havoc with airline security. I knew all along there was something suspicious about that too smooth layer of pristine marzipan with the fake holly on top. The dead weight—another giveaway. Thomas A. Smith Electric Rifle-cake. Charged raisins, tracking nuts, flammable-liquid-soaked peel. Just as well I didn't complicate things with Customs.

On the fifth day of Xmas, I make a trip downtown to shop. I actually find a few things for under the tree, the tree that I crossed off my list. Then I head down to the Love Nest—more like Looooove Nest—just saying it out loud is a turn-on. I find a stocking-stuffer vibrator for a fellow-MSer who no longer drives and hates shopping. She makes me feel so thankfully nimble. Her warm eyes say this could be you. Her cool hands say this will be you.

I choose purple because she likes violets. It's tiny, easy to use for those cool hands that can be uncooperative. I drop it off disguised as a package of hamburger so her granddaughter won't twig to the fact that she has a crush on herself and a cute new girly gadget. I think it's contagious this year. The crush. I bought myself the silver bullet keychain model. Not so girly. You never know. The pleasant surprise of my cell phone vibrating unexpectedly in my underwear is getting awkward if I stop to give somebody a lift. Nickleback tunes pouring from between my unreliable legs is uncomfortable for some hitchhikers. I don't get enough calls to make it worthwhile anyway. There is only one way to look at this—sexual.

I cross People SHOP off my list because I'll do the rest of the shopping on Boxing Day when it's cheaper, like for Noel and my cousin. Things that aren't explosive.

1. ~~People SHOP~~
2. Xmas dinner SHOP
3. ~~Cards~~
4. ~~Tree~~
5. ~~Ornaments~~   PHOTOS
6. ~~liquor~~
& 7. LIQUOR

On the sixth day of Xmas ... What can I say? Boredom. Tedious tasks. Yawn. Even X-ing takes too much energy.

On the seventh day of Xmas I spend half an hour of my Season's Greetings call on the phone listening to my Auntie Carole, who is younger than I am by one of those inexplicable family quirks. She's trying to decide if the tall dark erection pressed against her slow-dancing belly at the office party last night was a gentlemanly hard-on because he didn't have his hand on her ass, but more formally on her back. I'm wondering what difference it makes, seeing as he's a friend who is married to another woman, another friend (if I understand this right), when we're cut off. Her phone battery beeps and dies.

Wait a minute. Was that the guy she's been working for? The despicable bastard she'd been complaining about—like, for months? No. Couldn't be the same guy. I hope not. That would be the worst premeditated sex she could ever have. She would have to get herself drunk enough to finally end the last few years of creepy and tedious advances and fuck the boss after the Xmas party and be believably bad enough in bed, like comatose, no talk, no kissing on the mouth, to convince that power-player-Santa-baby to go home to the kids and never sexually harass her again because it's so convincingly not worth it. It's a dead end. And I do mean that sexually. Relieve the pressure in the process. Not even faking it.

I'll buy more liquor, right now while I have the cash. To have on hand. A bottle or two to accompany me to festivities. To toast the questionably "gentlemanly" hard-on. To toast getting cut off. To toast the really bad fuck and its effectiveness. I'm hungry enough to eat toast, and I never touch wheat. It's one of those dietary things that I've developed an MS aversion to. Last week I heard that a farmer with MS made a strange discovery. When he spread bird repellent in his wheat fields, it gave him a burst of energy. Go figure. Maybe Auntie Carole will agree to host a wheat-free dinner. I'll work on that.

1. ~~People SHOP~~
2. Xmas dinner SHOP
3. ~~Cards~~
4. ~~Tree~~
5. ~~Ornaments~~ PHOTOS
6. ~~liquor~~
& 7. LIQUOR

On the eighth day of Xmas I head out to a party. Through the large windows, I see it's packed with warm bodies. Co-hosted so I'll be guessing at who's who. There's an intriguing pile of shoes by the door, scarves, coats thrown over the railing. Add mine to the festive jumble and I'm in. Wine appears in my hand, a dozen candles warm my back on a table just the right leaning height. A leap of glow. A lean into glow. Do I really need more heat? I'm in the direct path to the kitchen so the parade past me is continuous. I'll eventually see pretty much everyone who's here without having to manoeuvre with the cane, which is an amazing feat with a glass of wine in your hand and a party around you.

I'm beginning to wonder if I'm at the wrong party. Everybody's a J: Jeannie, June, Jim, Jasmine, another Jeannie, Janet, and two John Carsons—two of them! Joe, the country crooner was here earlier but he didn't sing. I wonder if Jesus is on the guest list.

I wear my desire like a skin I can't shed, all-encompassing. Unfortunately, everything inside that skin is getting tired of the lean. There's only one chair left, a small wooden one, and it's all the way across the room. I'm not alone in wanting it. We eye each other across it. Then litigate with smiling eyes and share the seat. She's a brunette. Low-cut gorgeous in toasty pink. In family law. The friendly settlements, she says, and I like the fact she is not cutting hard-ass. Sweet, smart, a little older than I am but won't say how much. We argue with each other about who looks younger, better, long-suffering in the kindest way. We embellish each other.

"I saw you come in."

"You were radiant."

"I was hot," we both say, laughing, and it's true. And of course there had been the heat against my back from all the candles. And that smoldering internal combustion. Unquenchable. Is this Xmas cheer? Hormonal? Group chemistry? Holiday lust?

I want to hire her on the spot—legalize this minute, entwine her dark shoulder-length hair in mine. She makes me think of lamp-rubbing and magic.

I mention my separation moving in the divorce direction. She turns to me, suddenly serious, and says, "It might not be better, you know. Different isn't always better," and now I'm just scared. Scared of the attraction and too attracted to be scared. Scared to make the legal break, scared not to. What difference does legally alone make? I'm already desperate, so that wouldn't change. What's a relatively sane person to do? The chair we share is getting smaller. I tell her

I think I need to see her.

"In the office?" she asks.

Without answering her question, I kind of blurt, "Sometimes any difference is better than none." I mean the divorce, not her. I'm worried I'll start to stutter soon or drop my blue cheese and chili-honey down my shirt. Shit. Relax.

She reaches across my back with one arm and passes me a business card with the other, then quietly, "Just in case."

A hush spreads through the crowded room. People shuffle toward the walls to make room for something or somebody, and three kids from the neighbourhood fill the space made for them. It's hokey magic. I can't believe it. They start singing carols. They're dressed up like kings except one king looks too sweet, more like Cindy-Lou Who. She's the star, and she leads her backup well for her age. Eleven she says. Somebody (probably Cindy-Lou) passes around a pot, and it's filling up nicely. Then they disappear into the frosty night intent on their mission. Cindy-Lou wants to be an idol. More chairs arrive.

"This is my date," says my chair-sharer with slightly rolling eyes, and I wonder then why he's sitting here in his own chair on my right and she's moving away to a chair on my left. That's my bad side. His hand moves to my thigh to emphasize the punchlines of some pretty good jokes that I'll never remember. He's flashing Lee Marvin's off-screen set antics, and she's not laughing. He's a cameraman, he explains, so we get down to the transition between words and frames—whose tools are the most flexible, most powerful while retaining integrity, clarity. What is most accessible to the reader/viewer. The effect, the unexpected changes. The hand is warm, lively and reminds me of someone I can't put my finger on without a slap. I enjoy detached observation, sitting between the dating couple for just a moment. Then she suddenly droops. They exchange glances.

"You're tired," he says to her, resigned accusation. Low-cut-gorgeous-in-pink bumps her weary head on the chandelier as she gets up out of the chair and leaves with her date. Although it's a mouth worthy of dreaming, hers isn't the mouth I'll dream about this damn eighth night. What a shame.

On the ninth day of Xmas, while the party's still on, precisely on the decoratively antiqued townhouse stroke of one, I find a soulmate, a smoking buddy. This is a woman who not only smokes but is willing to carry my bottle of wine as we shuffle (I cautiously tap) across the icy patio to two wrought-iron chairs frozen solidly to the cement. My yellow lighter does the trick for a pair of Players stubbies, way too strong Regular by mistake, but they taste just right coming from the Players Extra Light package I slid them into. Lesser crime.

"I've been wanting to find you all night. John told me all about you." (Who the hell is John? I wonder.) "So? We have good friends in common. And you write, eh? So, what do you write?"

I love this question. What is it she really wants to know? Does she really care? She's probably a writer. Everybody here is a writer, even the lawyer and the cameraman. Does she want to compare writing notes? Just want to talk? I'm guessing this new relationship is one where I can remain speechless. She'll answer for me. Here we go.

"I'm Ruby. Ruby Oswald. Yah, American, too. Can you imagine growing up like that? On the dark side, for damn sure. It's a name I can't leave behind, though. A promise to my grandmother before she died. Before Kennedy and all that." My smoking buddy looks into my face with one eye squeezed shut and passes me the bottle of red. "We could be family, you know. It's the freckles."

It's true. We could be closely related, our noses finely sprayed with the rust colour of dried blood on a white bathroom mat. We could be shaded and dotted with the same cinnamon crayon, shivering, blowing smoke and warm breath up into the blue-lit LED-streaked night.

"But that's not the real problem," she continues, having already lost the inevitable thread of genetic connection. At least a 98.6 percent chance no matter who the hell we are.

A short man with frothy dark brows (John, I'm guessing) slides the patio door open, hisses in silhouette, "Assassin," and slides the door shut. Maybe not John. Maybe not friend.

She snorts, moves away from the comment. "The problem—and this is so hard to talk about. Oh, fuck. Maybe I should have taken their names. Maybe it was a curse." She's tearing up now, wiping at her eyes with the back of her hand. "The problem, y'see, is that my boyfriends keep dying, even my ex-husbands, four in the last year." She fights off sobs. Collects herself. Drinks from the bottle. Takes an extended drag on her cigarette.

"With you or without you?" I ask, forced into speech, heartless. Well into our second bottle of wine, I'm loosely wondering if I'm safe out here with my new sister on the frozen patio, and knowing I can't run away.

"Without," she says staring without expression, not needing any further explanation for the question. Some things are perceived with more clarity after a great deal of booze. So I decide the word "without" is a secret message, a dismissive missive, for my unconscious desire. Maybe I am safe and I should just keep quiet and do without, too, in a sexual way.

"One husband, the second, had a bad liver. They found him in his house with two hundred, no, not quite, one hundred and ninety-two empty vodka bottles, and he had no will. It was Stolichnaya. We used to drink it together, toast each other, but not so much, you know. His third wife and all our kids—there are five of them—are fighting over his company."

"He had no will! He'd be bad company, anyway." I have the

nerve, the gall, to laugh. Did I guffaw? (What a word!) And she has enough humour or desperation to laugh too.

"No, his business company. You're kidding, right?"

Someone should kick me in my good leg. I don't deserve to still be standing. I deserve to go home alone, without.

"My last boyfriend, Zane, had a heart attack. The love of my life, Kenny, his car hit a pole. About halfway up. He thought he was flying. Now there was a fucking angel."

What difference does fucking make anyway when you're an angel? This reminds me, for some reason, of a sex-toy party I went to a few years ago. For the ice-breaker, I was paired up with a woman in her early sixties. I drew a question out of a brown paper bag: "Where is the funniest place you ever had sex?" and she answered so honestly it was painful. "I've never had sex, funny or otherwise." Now, that's a shock. Nothing funny about it. I'd tell my freckled, possibly familially related sister-friend-soulmate this relatively stunning story but she's still describing her year. Four. Wow. I should be more compassionate. A better listener. I have no heart by the second bottle of wine. No beat if I don't go in and warm up.

Ruby Oswald ties my scarf in a Paris knot while I try to kiss away a too-drunk-to-drive-versus-taxi argument between really old friends. She walks me out to my car, scrapes my windows while I lean through one last cigarette. We laugh and someone, a curly-haired woman, yells at us to shut up from the townhouse window, open yapping, hollow rapping on the double-glazing, above the parking lot. My Ruby sister tells me I have great legs, which is pretty hysterical because they're working way less than even usual by this time. Plus the fact that I'm bundled up, layered up like a snowman. No matter what she says about my legs or how well she ties my scarf, hers isn't the mouth I dream about that night.

On the tenth day of Xmas I watch two movies back to back. Sip on a little Southern Comfort. Read the paper. Smoke a non-medicinal, non-government-approved joint. Find my horoscope. It says spend some time with my main squeeze. I love that term. Maybe it was good to stay home. Lay low. Well, okay, the rest is easy. I've had a crush on myself for a while now. Months, at least. Well, I guess I'm it. I light candles, put on The Doors, but the rest of the date doesn't go so well. I'm too tired and too wasted to bother seriously, generously with my body, and I end up feeling cheap and headachy. I'm not very good company—just frustrated, pissed off. I'm this close ... this close to release, but for some reason this particular orgasm is eluding me. Jesus. Is this another physical failure? Sinistral or sinister? Whole body? Mind? Paranoia prevails. Well, at least I can wake up by myself in the morning. I'll read until ... oh, just one more pee before I turn the reading light out. I may have to count sheep. Meditate as shepherd.

But there it is again in the narrow column of brightness pouring through the bathroom skylight. My body. Not thin, but hungry. Touch-starved. Not beautiful. Flawed. Scarred. But truly familiar. Not reliable in the least, but in this surreal light, a hopeful friend. This radiant illumination draws my eye up through the celestially friendly plexiglas bubble to a glorious and ecstatic star, far brighter than the thumbnail moon.

I step back into shadow, lean against the counter, my back to the mirror, admire the heavens, the starlight, and take pleasure in the clear definition of the Arborite edge, the horizontal pressure, the cool sharp against my butt. My instinctive fingers' gentle flutter of encouragement reminds me to be patient. The stroke of chimes from the old clock in the cupboard spells be kind. This will be pure me. No gadgets or books. Sweet to my friendly body. Straight up. Honest. Standing has always been the best, anyway. Just to see if I can bring myself to my knees. It's a revelation. An epiphany. Enlightenment. And before I know it, before I know it

Six Degrees of Altered Sensation

I'm absolutely—absolutely—holy—wholly—

there.

It is a

fucking

(well almost)-

miracle.

The best.

The best.

The best.

I stand my ground. Hold on to the coming until the star has drifted almost out of rectangular sight. Knees buckle but I stay on my feet. I swear t'gawd, I smell incense or frankincense or something. I hear bells. Oh, no. It's some ass ringing the doorbell. I'll ignore that. Smoke a Camel (or a Players). Turn and kiss my face in the mirror. And there they are, the lips I'll dream about, a little thin but sensitive. Subtle lips. Kiss my cool mirror lips. Chilled like white wine. Merry sweet Xmas, nothing X-rated about it. Maybe I'm already dreaming. And I do mean that in a way that can only be sexual.

Who said there had to be twelve days, anyway?

~~1. People SHOP~~
~~2. Xmas dinner SHOP~~
~~3. Cards~~
~~4. Tree~~
~~5. Ornaments~~   PHOTOS
~~6. liquor~~
& 7. LIQUOR

Chicken in Mourning

"Chicken in Mourning," the recipe reads, and as I read it, a part of me wants to weep. For the beginning of unrest. For the end of a beginning. This is a recipe for change. I can feel it in the act of rinsing this raw chicken in my kitchen sink, emptying its body cavity, patting it dry, inside and out. I can feel it in the blast of Bif Naked's *Purge* CD. And there's the phone. Oh, shit. Wash my hands.

"Hello?"

"Hi, Mel," says the familiar voice. Familiar, like fifteen years' worth of hellos, highs and lows.

"Hi, John. What's up?" I'm suspicious of rejection. Ready to argue, cajole, arm-twist through the phone line.

"Are you okay? You sound funny."

"I'm fine. It's just allergies or something," I lie, embarrassed to be emotional over poultry. Over anything. "Just don't tell me you're not coming."

"Uh, I'm not coming."

"Why the hell not? You said this was a good day. Seriously. You said … "

"Hang on. I'm just kidding, sort of. I can't make it for dinner. I have to drop my brother at the airport. But I can get there by about nine. Is that too late to bother? Should I just skip it?"

"No, just come. Just come whenever. Jackie's bringing her new boyfriend—the one from the internet dating thing. You know. That poor guy, Paul, I think Paul is his name, will be alone with three women. He may need some support, a little testosterone backup just to hold his own, so to speak."

"Okay, okay. I'll come by about nine then." His laughing makes me smile. Then he remembers, "Are you sure you don't need a ride to the clinic? What time is your appointment? I can still take you, you know."

"No, really. I told you, that's my business. I'll manage fine. I always have. See you at nine."

"You bet." Click. I do the same, wondering how we've been friends for so long without spoiling it with sex in one of those sloppy-drunk desperate moments. We've joked about it, sure, but never talked about it. It's just there. The boundary. The barrier. Stay out of the bedroom.

Back to my recipe and my first seriously generous host-type dinner in my new place. Not pizza. Still sharing but not potluck-pity-moving kind of stuff. I used to love to cook. Ahh. Maybe I still do. This recipe is written in such a sensuous way that I don't know, through still blurry eyes, whether to be famished or aroused. Look at this. Read it. Slide your fingers under the breast skin, it says. Overlap layers of black truffles, sliced paper thin with a mandoline, under the skin. I had to look that up, the mandoline. Of course, it has to do with sharps and flats but there's nothing melodious about it but its name, just an adjustable razor-sharp blade. It's like the slicer-dicer advertised on the shopping channel. Which would you rather use? Mandoline sounds so much sexier and truffle-appropriate. But I don't have either, so a pair of paring knives will have to do.

I tenderly place the dark aromatic slices under the skin, across the breast (breasts), along the leg. It actually says to tuck a couple of slices along the inside of the thigh. Then I turn the bird and slip in more, down near the neck. Or where a neck would be, should be.

Charlene's coming tonight and she has a beautiful neck, a few springy ringlets always evading elastic capture, sassy blonde bun enhancing her height. A tall attitude, that woman. She always brings veggies, long lean carrots, string beans, English cucumber. Freudian pods and peels. The husband stays away. She'll give my poultry a pass, too, at dinner—too meaty, too avian.

I have to remember not to let slip the fact that I bounced a cheque for the truffles. She'll pull out her financial-advisor bag of tricks. Tut-tut me as if I'm irredeemable. Like an outdated coupon. Tell me how to live hopefully so I can enjoy life later, but what about now? If I followed her every monetary instruction, in fact, I could afford to get my car towed home from the bar when I can't walk or drive, just like she does. Regularly. Religiously, I think, but don't press for details. Charlene points out that you get a warm ride home, your car to wake up to in the morning, and no admission of liquor-related guilt to your friends.

Looking down at the bird, my Chicken in Mourning, I envision the dark French veil truffled, ruffled under its skin that will be golden, crisp, translucent. A beautiful chicken widow with a dusky mantilla trailing to her footless ankles. A delectable bird. I can almost taste her.

The fine art of trussing is next. I follow the detailed instructions carefully. Slip the string under the bird above the legs, pull the ends along the breasts, the tail, the wingtips, pull snugly to the body, wrap three times. Ritualistic. Black truffle magic. Maybe it works like a spell. Maybe I should tear the word SEX out of the newspaper or write out my vexation on parchment and insert it in the widow's body before baking. Send a steamy message up through the stove vent to a literate spirit. It makes me shiver. Don't mess with magic. Bad karma. Might backfire.

I put my chicken in the fridge, slap on my face, grab my coat. I'll rest my legs on the drive. Rejuvenate.

I remember going to this same MS clinic for my annual checkup, not the first time, but later, like a couple of years after I was given an official MRI name for my condition. I was shocked when I walked into the waiting room. Most folks were older, parked between caregivers, canes, metal walkers—a constrained herd huddled near the magazine rack. I thought *good*, no young ones here struggling to be able. Then I thought *bad* at having to deal with this unpredictable disease so many more years. No receptionist at her welcome post. I sat down. Anxiety. Angst. I remember thinking, wow, there's a lot I don't know about MS.

When the receptionist showed up, I headed to the counter. I felt all those waiting faces swing in curious unison to watch my territorial negotiations. If I could have jerked my head around fast without falling, I'd have given them the look. If I had been on my way out and had no underwear on ... oh, never mind.

"Can I help you?" name-tagged Mary had asked.

"I have an appointment with Dr. Sharni for two o'clock."

"Dr. Sharni? For the MS Clinic?"

"Yes. That's right." A swipe of uncertainty. Shit. What now? Don't tell me he's not here, I thought.

"He's not here," Mary said, picking up her chiming phone, hello, hello, then, hold please, cradling the ergonomically correct beige receiver into the knitted blue hollow of her turtleneck. "I mean, this isn't the MS Clinic."

"But this is the MS clinic. This is where I always come. Has it moved?" There was something I wasn't getting. I could no longer trust name-tagged Mary. I felt a flush. I was pinking up like Mary's lipstick. The eyes on my back were becoming downright intrusive. "I know I've been here." Maybe my reality wasn't a shared one. Uncooperatively solipsistic. I was losing my mind. Maybe I should have gotten down on my hands and knees right there, right then, and looked for it under the counter because it sure as hell felt like it had shrunk to the size of a peppercorn and fallen out my ear and rolled far, far away.

"Usually," says Mary, "but it's Tuesday." (I wanted to scream, "*And your point being?*") but she, oh so complacently, went on to explain, "Today is the Alzheimer's Clinic. We share the space on alternate days. Are you sure it's not the Alzheimer's you wanted?"

Want, Mary dearest? I was struck dumb, relieved, somehow, to have survived the conversation, but dumb. Disorganized. Stupid. Forgetful. Wait a minute, no. I was annoyed. Mad. Pissed off. Somebody screwed it up, told me the wrong day.

"There must be some mistake." I dug in my purse for my reminder card, something I did strangely trust, as if a specific combination of symbols could erase every other identity, mistaken or not, from that waiting room. There was a mistake. Mine. "Oh," I said. Just oh, and I tried to walk out with some sort of dignity, but I seemed to have forgotten that too. The waiting room scene took on meaning—some were agitated because they didn't understand. Others distressed because they did. Maybe I really did belong to the Alzheimer's Clinic, I thought. Thought seriously. Then hysterically, as I walked past the sign in the lobby, "Alzheimer's Clinic today."

I am really lucky, I thought, I only have the MS mess. I still trusted that I knew (unlike small boys and my "Altzed" uncle) that it wasn't cool to sway around with hands in pants, like on the bus, in tranced public waltzing. It's all in the knowing. But I had to admit, no, it's me who suffers, not them, stifled by societal strictures. Like a socially trussed chicken widow. Like the bird I trust almost enough to consider for a supernatural tryst.

"Melanie. Melanie Farrell." I'm back in the present, reverie broken. I hear my name, look up, and there he is. The compassionate, quietly smiling Dr. Sharni, always a blue shirt, navy tie. This is one of those places I never cry. It's my rule, my role here, and I am good. I follow him down the hall to his office. The guy always makes me feel like I'm part of a special club. He knows my history, my medical cartography, confessed personal interests from my chart, but he's so smooth that I can pretend that he remembers me from last year. That I stand out and maybe I do because I can still stand at all.

"So, Melanie, you're looking great. How are things? Still writing? Going to school?" he asks, settling back in his swivel chair for a comfy chat. I want to hug him. Squeeze him in his swivel chair. Let him pat my back while I tell him how good everything is.

I'm almost at ease but trying to keep my adrenaline up so I can show him, prove to him that I am no worse. "Great, actually. Yah, I'm still writing. Not so much schooling." (Dropped my courses during the big move but won't go there with Dr. Sharni, today. Too openly stressful. Sign of dysfunction.) "Not much change physically. I've needed the cane, haven't been able to do without it at all in the last year." But I'm quick to reassure him before he drops his compassionate chin. "Actually some things are better." I fail, again, to mention I'm living on my own. Retain information control. Reticent disclosure. He assumes I mean physically.

"Well, good. Let's take a walk then," says Dr. Sharni. This is my cue. The performance. He stands in the doorway (upstage left), holding my cane, watching me progress, veer, careen all the way down the carpeted hall (downstage), trying to ignore, hide, overpower my progressive disease. He meets me with my cane before I'm halfway back, and I know that's not a good sign. (No applause, either.) But he says an upbeat, "Uh-huh," before we head back into his office, he to his notes, my file, my life now, me to the exam table. I know this routine. Don't need prompts.

I lounge against the table, bracing myself for the fear-factor-trust-test. It's a lot like those team exercises where you let your trusting self fall back into the arms of your sincerely waiting teammates. Only this time, I don't have to consciously fall back. I only have to stand still and close my eyes. The falling happens without my knowing. I can't tell I'm moving through air, until my only teammate, Dr. Sharni, grips my arms to stop me and my eyes fly open, recognizing the magnitude of this flaw. I survive. Get control. Slow my heart, not from the feeling of falling but from the lack of it. Without my eyes, I am incapable of erection, not an erection but uprightness.

"Hm-mm," my teammate doctor acknowledges, then notates, and motions me onto the table. I get rid of my shoes, climb up, swing my legs while he writes more illegible notes, data, information, in-formation, about deformed me.

We move into the second act. This is the least uncomfortable but the most difficult, not physically but because the soft touch of his fingers brushing, stroking my cheeks, so softly, brings up an ache of the longing, the magnitude almost insurmountable. He asks, "How's the sensation here? Anything different?" I want to draw his fingers into my mouth with my tongue. But I don't, of course. I follow the script. Keep my tongue in my mouth, my thoughts in my head.

Then, "Cover one eye. Follow my finger," he says and my eyes, one at a time, follow as dutifully as they can. Then taking my right hand, he places it near his shoulder, but instead of asking me to dance, he lets go, says "Okay, touch your nose." This sounds too easy and it is, but wait. When I switch to my left, the difficulty is always ridiculously beyond belief—a scary hesitation, my digit searching its memory bank for placement. The index finger on my left hand has forgotten where my nose is. How is that even possible? Somewhere between my brain and the tip of my finger, the distance has been skewed, proprioception—that crucial sensory connection—in disarray.

Then he taps my elbows, knees for reflex. The "bad" side is always a fascination. It seems logical to me that there would be little response along with little feeling, numb tingling, but in fact, the left knee flings up the lower leg with such ferocity it could be detrimental to Dr. Sharni if he were less wary, more weary.

We go through all the strength tests. In various positions I pull, he pushes or he pulls and I push. And I play hard to prove

I still can. He does the "Babinsky." This is the creepy one where he scrapes a stick or a key (I kid you not) up the bottom of my foot, heel to toe. Nothing to do with dancing but it does give the foot a certain newborn curl.

Then we move into the sharpy challenges. He pokes my extremities repeatedly with a long pin. I respond with "Sharp" or "Pressure" unless I can't feel it at all, in which case I remain mute wondering what the hell is taking him so long to find a good sharply painful place.

"There is some improvement, actually. That's great!" he says, adding notes to my file. I have succeeded in pleasing him.

"Enough to slide me down the scale?" I ask. I'm talking about the Krutzky Disability Status Scale. I hate this scale, this code, this cipher, but always ask. Need to know. Did I change? I want a better number. I want to be luckier. I want to be less.

"No. Sorry, Melanie. You're still at six. But that's a good thing."

"So, I'm still closer to ten than zero." Closer to death than symptom-free. Closer to death by MS. In fact, I'm five points, half-the-freakin'-scale away from where I was ten years ago. This is always a sobering moment. The one I want to handle well. Why do I always ask?

"Hmm. Five would feel better." As close as I can get to acknowledgement.

"I know," he says, always gently, "but six is a huge area on this particular scale. Anyway, we know the scale is flawed. Just, well, no one's come up with a better way of measuring disability. It's difficult to knit together all eight neuro-systems."

I try and remember the flawed list of eight. *Cerebral. Visual. Cerebellar.* That sounds like Jellicle from the musical, "Cats." My poetic mind shifts into gear while Dr. Sharni writes up my life file. *Brainstem.* Reminds me of gardening. I wanted to grow Graceful, row after row of it in my garden, an abundance of brain flowers on fragile stems against the porch steps at my feet. Damn. What were the others? Oh, yah, *pyramidal. Bowel and bladder*, how could I forget that one? *Sensory.* Sensual, sexual.

"Things seem really good." He has that ever optimistic tone in his positive voice so I'll follow his lead, relieved, put an up look on my face. "There's one other thing we should talk about," he goes on.

"Something new to try, you mean?" I've been pretty game so far. Tried the steroids, a few different drugs, a few hundred injections. Hell, I even tried rubbing ostrich oil into my skin but I got tired of smelling like turkey dinner. Kitty loved it though. We (Dr. Sharni and I remain a team) just haven't found the perfect potion yet. Scorpion venom is the latest thing. I read that it was the new high in Hong Kong, not an MS blocker. Maybe not a bad thing. "Scorpion venom might be more fun than the bee sting therapy."

"Scorpions aren't that far along in the research yet. There's nothing new. I think you've pretty much had a chance at everything that we've got so far. I'll make sure and let you know, though, if anything promising comes up. There are always studies." *But I'm already at six.*

Dr. Sharni goes on, "Speaking of studies, we got the results back from the Sexual Neuro-Response study."

"That was a weird one. Don't think I'd do that one again." Genital hookup. Simulated stimulation. Lab libido. Occupational orgasm.

"You requested the results. Do you still want to know how the study went?"

"Sure," I say but I feel suddenly anxious, like, why would he double-check? Protocol? "Is there something I need to know?"

"No. No. Nothing life-threatening or anything like that. But the data collected from you does show that you will only be able to have a few more orgasms before your sensory nerves, the sympathetic system will stop responding. According to your file you've had a pretty inactive or lost libido for quite some time, since the onset, really. It's common with MS. We've talked about it." He's beginning to look a bit concerned as he tries to read me.

I keep a straight face while I digest this for all of ten seconds. Then decide the course I'll take. That lovely libido was found during the last few months. In fact it was never lost. Just subdued, suffocated, hidden, and nothing to do with MS, although they had me believing it for years. Dr. Sharni wouldn't know that, of course. Well then, I'll just turn it off again. Shut it down. It's been fun but there are more important things in life. Really.

"Oh, is that all? You had me worried for a minute," I say, thinking he'll never know. In the big picture, that's no big loss. People lose it all the time. "Can they really measure that? I thought this whole MS thing was unpredictable. Pretty weird. A real measurement." I sift back in time through the study questionnaires: age, gender, time of MS onset, blah, blah, blah. Maybe they *can* quantify me.

"It's the only area of the body they've been able to successfully use the testing on. The number they've given you is six. You have six orgasms. In fact they cut the study short, the outcome was so successful. The accuracy I mean. That's why you're able to have the results so quickly. It's amazing really."

"Right. Amazing. Now we just need something equally amazing to get rid of the MS." I put my shoes back on. *But every orgasm is so different, with its own personality, an erotic entity.* "Six, you say? Absolutely six?"

"Well I suppose it could be seven but six is the number I see here. If you're worried about this, want to talk to someone, we can line up an appointment with Ruth, the psychologist here. I think you've met with her before." Maybe he does remember me.

"I don't think I need to see a psychologist. Ruth, right?" (*Rhymes with truth.*) "It's fine, really. I'm just curious, though. Is this orgasm, this number six thing anything to do with my number six on the Kurtzky scale?"

"No," he says with a quiet laugh, trying to take this to a lighter level. I can feel my time's almost up. My turn's over. "Just coincidence," he reassures me, pushing himself up to standing.

"Anyway," I go on, "I'm relieved it's nothing worse and the cane, well, I'm almost used to needing it."

"You manage just fine with it. And they are working on the research. Something may come up. Keep in touch." Dr. Sharni sees me to the door, resting his hand against my shoulder blade.

"Thanks." Why do I always say thanks, no matter what? "See you in a year." What a weird relationship. *Keep in touch.*

It's the touch word that sticks with me as I weave back out through the waiting room and finally to the sanctuary of my car. My comforting old car. Van, really, but I call it a car to piss off touchy automotarians. Touchy. *Touch.* But as I pull into heavy traffic, the word I can't shake is SIX.

By the time I get home from the MS clinic, park my car-sanctuary-van, pick up the newspaper and get in the door, I'm MS-exhausted. Still trying to think tough instead of touch. Life is too fucking bizarre. I'll have a drink or six. SIX. I'll put my feet up, even the good one. I carry the wine bottle under my arm, my favourite glass in hand, the orange one, the biggest, and the corkscrew in my pocket. *Settle down*, I think, as I lean back into the couch. I should buy this wine by the case so I don't have to go to the liquor store so often. They're starting to call me by name.

I really can't let this orgasm thing bother me. The latent stress of the post-clinic reality strangles me. The thought of people, guests, overwhelms me. It's too late to pull out, call off the dinner. These friends would understand, but stubborn pride demands another performance. I don't really want to be alone anyway. I know myself at least that well. I always resort to sorting my life out in a crowd. Takes the edge off.

Maybe I should have ordered that Swedish wallpaper—the

cocktail party in a twenty-foot pre-pasted roll. My living room would be papered with haphazardly placed, life-sized, very quiet, nonjudgmental paper dolls, some solo, others in random groupings. Stock-market suits intermingled with little black dresses or après-ski with high-tech gear, authentic sweaters. Maybe a costume party. Oh, man. Reminds me of that Goth party. I can't for the life of me forget that girl with the black star nipples or the pale powdered vampire with the ten-inch Zippo, cock to match, in his makeup kit. Kiss imposters were necking on the four-way bench in the two-way corner by the bifold doors. And I sat there holding court, at the head of the smoking table, a martinied matriarch with a powderless bag-o-tricks. Feels like another life but it's not. It's all greedily mine.

    I have an hour. One hour. Why did I think I could do this dinner easily? Breezily, even? My chicken widow is still mourning in the fridge. The guests are coming about six. *Six.* "Let it go," I warn myself out loud, feeling powerless. It's just that I can't control someone else's restrictive number. I'll make it mine—the number six. Take it over. Take it on. Bring it on. No, that's what I don't want. Yet. My limited number of orgasms. Orgasms Ltd. What if I can't prove them wrong? The need, the want, the Desire with a capital "D" that I *can* control. Have always controlled. Well, okay, maybe occasionally, consciously chose not to. Back up a few months. I didn't care. Years. There was more to life. A decade. Not worth remembering. So why now just months before I get an official orgasmic number, like the remainder at the end of long division, this sudden interest, desperate lust, fascination with all things faintly sexual? Remotely sensual? Ironic unfairness. And that blatantly meaningful curled symbol 6. Six is so close to sex, even the numerical becomes hotly erotic. That scorching number is everywhere, let me tell you. Channel 6. Page 6. February 6, open a 26er. I'll go and clear off the table, get slowly busy. Occupied. Preoccupied.

Let's see. We need all *six* chairs.

The microwave reads 5:36 when I hear the doorbell, but people are always ringing the doorbell here, so I wait 'til I hear voices. Voices that I recognize. Jackie's got a key. So I don't have to get up in case I can't. Why is she always early? I think it's an anti-social personality flaw. Goes against the grain, the chaff. Chafes me.

"Come on in," I call vaguely toward the door. The decision to cancel is out of my hands. It'll be great. Good, at least. It always is. I'll get seriously cheery. It's either buck up or fuck up—both of which I've had considerable experience with. I'll go with the former. Form the mood. Shape the evening. Share the load.

"It's just us, Mel." I hear the slight question between assurance and reassurance, coded warning, in Jackie's voice. She has someone with her. Oh, right, the date. Paul. She's just making sure I'm not doing anything untoward, too forward or backward, too strange for a stranger.

"Jackie. You're finally here," I half-joke and she gives me a glance, an aside, before bustling her food and drink out of the arms of her attractively patient, quietly awkward fellow-traveller and into my kitchen, which suddenly becomes her kitchen. It's our arrangement and I'm happy to acquiesce. Give up this culinary control. She diminishes my recently acquired inadequacy as only a good friend can. I face the new man. "I guess you've figured out I'm Melanie, Mel if you like. You must be Paul," I say, smiling, balancing against the counter and reaching out my hand to take his much warmer one.

"Actually, I'm Marvin." He's still holding my hand. I'm trying to get my head around the switch-up, recover my manners (or somebody's), and figure out why that name tickles something in my memory. Marvin has become an unusual name, along with Maurice, Debbie, Agnes, Frank. Norman's fallen out of the range of normal, too. More like my dad's generation, but this man's definitely not from that era. Sounds like a Pompano Beach bar, I think. Marvin's Bar and Grill.

"Sorry, uh, Marvin. My mistake." I'm trying to smooth things here. Doing it badly.

"Yah, Mel has a short memory." Jackie pipes up, but she's the one who's got a baby blush-on. She's avoiding my eyes so I'll cover for her again with another of my own newly ascribed endless shortcomings. We're even, Jackie and I.

"The chicken's in the fridge. I was thinking when you got here 'she' could go in, but I haven't made it as far as the oven yet. Would you mind, Jackie? New recipe. Take care with her. She's special: 375 degrees, convection. Oh, scrap convect. That was another life. Another oven. She needs a baste every ten minutes." My horoscope said delegate. "Marvin, could you pour some wine? The bottle's by the couch. Unless you'd prefer something else. Beer's in the fridge. Glasses are here," I say, pointing in the general direction of the cupboards. I like to see how people deal with a new situation, especially in my territory. I'm not mean or anything. It's just that everyone has their own brand of ownership of foreign space. Marvin seems curious. As though he expected something better. I sense relief.

"Jackie, who the hell is Marvin? And what happened to Paul?" I hiss, leaning toward her ear.

She ignores my question. Answers me with another. "She? You're calling our dinner 'she'? Charlene won't like that. Too personal. Too gendered." Then to Marvin, off fetching the wine, "Wine for me too, please."

"It's the recipe. It's called Chicken in Mourning," I attempt to explain my avian relationship. "Charlene won't eat it anyway. I don't mean the chicken's a 'she' like a puck—shoot her in, or a truck—park her over there. It's the recipe." The writing, the wording, the mood of the mourning letters on the page this morning.

Six Degrees of Altered Sensation

Jackie pulls the veiled main course out of the fridge, mumbling some affirmation. Marvin refills my glass and I can't help but notice two thumbs on his left hand. In opposition. Proposition. New position.

Marvin's hand holding out my wineglass triggers this kick-ass curiosity. I'm trying not to stare. Marvin has a pair of opposing thumbs on his left hand. I mean, they look perfect—a mirror image. Just imagine the double smudge of round whorls against, well, say, the stretch nipple to nipple, sliding down my belly. A shock of attraction erupts. Inexorably, insensibly linked. We share a port-side flaw. Hell, we share a left synchronicity, a sinistral affinity. Hysterically numerically, liberally connected. That makes six digits. Six. And my magic number as of today, the big S-I-X. A gift I didn't want from my neurologist in Room 616 at the MS clinic, six on the disability scale (not a good thing, remember) and six clinically prognosticated orgasms left in my (apparently) clinically non-libidinous life—information my friends know nothing, nada, nyet about. Yet.

I notice the knuckle of one shapely outer thumb bend just around the bottom of the glass's tall-stemmed base. The other, the inner thumb, stretches high, almost to the rim, and in between, Marvin's fingers (all four of them) cup my wine. I can imagine the full stretch of that hand just about anywhere on my body. I know what I have to do.

"I'm going to Climax," I blurt. The only sounds after Jackie's laugh (more of a snort), then her clutched intake of breath, are the doorbell and Charlene's voice.

"Sorry? What?" Marvin's moved away from me slightly but still offers the wine, unsure whether to keep an eye on me or on the opened front door.

"Hey," Charlene calls from the door. "Sorry I'm late." Then, "Anybody here?"

Jackie answers by the time Charlene hits the kitchen, "Well, some of us are more here than others." She looks from me to Marvin and back to me. Then she throws the question out sideways. "Marvin, what did she say?" As if he had somehow pulled a fast one on her. But she didn't skip a beat, didn't let him speak. "Mel, what did you say? What are you talking about? No, never mind. Just repeat what you said. Maybe I didn't hear that."

I take the wine from Marvin, just brushing that extra thumb. Is he smiling?

"I said I'm going to Climax. It's suddenly crucial that I do this," I say looking into their wide eyes, one pair at a time. "Yah, Climax."

Marvin finally finds his voice, makes a noise, "Would you like a hand with that?"

"Mel, are you losing it or what?"

"That's what I'm trying to do. Not lose it. Yup, Climax. Climax, Saskatchewan." And I feel a shift in the room. "Relax. I'll tell you in a minute. Hey, Charlene. Good to see you."

Jackie keeps staring. "Are you nuts? You just moved into this place, Mel." Jackie takes her eyes off me long enough to do a flip introduction. "Charlene, Marvin. Marvin, Charlene. Marvin's pouring, Char," and she passes our man, Marvin, a wine glass out of the cupboard knowing her friend's drinking preference.

"Jackie, my friend, I have a plan. Don't worry. I'll explain. Let's just get dinner on the road here." On the road, travel, movement, migration. Yes, the draw is there, the idea is pulling me now.

"Jesus, Mel, you can't just ... It's going to get worse, you know."

"Oh, just fuck off. What do you do that for? I know. Just cut it out. Don't think limitations. Think synchronous opportunity. I know I can't walk much. I know it'll get worse. Fuck, I know I have MS. I just have to do some things. There's a week-long writers' retreat in Climax, Saskatchewan. There must be a way. Charlene, Marvin's poured you a glass of wine while I've been blathering."

Did I just say blathering? Like lathering. Soap. Slippery. Marvin.

"Marvin, welcome to the club."

"Hey, I'm just glad to be here. I don't want to ..."

"You know what. You'll know way more about me by the end of the night, so let's just pretend that we've already known each other for a very long time. Jackie's laid everything on the table but our dinner. Let's drink to you, Marvin, our newest member. This is another beginning of some ... well, we'll see. Adventure?"

"Christ, Mel. Can't get a word in edgewise." Charlene has found her voice. "Thanks, Jackie," she says, swirling her glass, always cool. "Marvin, that's your name right, Marvin? Well, let's make a toast to you, Marvin. Being the long-lost newbie." And Char, Jackie, Marvin and I all lift our glasses, clink, sip. And that rich red slides down our throats, warms us. The evening becomes an entity and we're each some small but crucial part of it.

Marvin steps up. "Thanks, Charlene. Ladies. Or women. It's an honour to be here, somehow. I mean I feel like I belong or something. You guys make me feel really kind of normal."

We all hoot, agree, pat each others' arms, backs, well, okay, maybe a thumb or two, but hey, who's checking. The timer goes. The kitchen is calling but, thankfully, not to me. All I have to do is tilt my head toward the table and Marvin's right there. The man with two left thumbs on one side of me, my cane on the other. It's a wacky balance but it works.

My mouth is out of control, running on ahead of logic. I say to Marvin, "What beautiful, uh, thumbs, er, hands. Hand. Digits ... I mean, uh, you have six digits on your left hand, which is really quite unusual ..."

"I've noticed, Mel." Marvin has a sense of humour. Seems to be enjoying my awkward moment. Decides to release me from it by moving toward the table and asking, "Your wine? Do you want me to put it here? Are you ready to sit down?"

I am so ready. I sit down, park my cane in its usual corner, but my mouth carries on. "Very attractive, actively. I mean actually. Well, a hand tells a lot about a man, symbolizes so many things— even the whole French thing, you know, *le main*. Gawd, sorry, Marvin. I didn't mean to embarrass you. I just think you have a lovely hand ... hands ... "

"It's okay. Really. My hand is flattered."

He leaves his hand resting near my glass. Is he nervous? I ignore the glass, take my eyes off Marvin's thumbs and plant them on his face. Not bad. Not bad at all. Better by the minute. There's a gloss on his forehead. A burnish on dark wood. Fullish lips. Eyes deep enough to drown yourself in.

"Excuse me, uh, Marvin. There's something I have to do." I head off into the kitchen, without the cane (screw it) and just hang onto the counter as I go. I'm on a mission. Should I feel guilty yet? Is he just friendly flirty? Better tread carefully. Yikes, it's warm in here.

I scribble "6" on a turquoise post-it, bypass Jackie and Charlene at the sink and go directly to the oven, open the door and shove the crumpled paper between the chicken's curvaceously plump legs. Then I text John—Don't come. Early bed.

"Hey Mel," Jackie says, over her shoulder with her hands full of lettuce, "the bird's coming along nicely."

"Yes indeed. Everything seems to be coming together."

"Where's the butter, Mel?" Charlene asks, "and parsley?"

"In the fridge, I hope. Compartment in the door?" I head back to the table, to Marvin, to his hands. "So, Marvin, you've known Jackie long?"

"We actually met at the video store a couple of months ago. The one down on Highland and James."

"Oh, right. I know the place." (Christ, they've got a movie connection. I should have known.)

I light the candles. What was I thinking, anyway? That damn attraction thing was so strong but there's no way I'll mess with Jackie's date, boyfriend, mate. Poaching is out of the question.

"We have a mutual friend, Paul," Marvin goes on.

"Oh, sorry. What did you say?" I'd better pay attention but drop the lighter. I'm missing something, sidetracked by the Bic.

Marvin leans over to pick it up. "Paul. Have you met Paul?"

"No. No, I ... "

"Well, Paul is a friend of mine and a friend of Jackie's ... "

"Now I'm confused. Is Paul ... I mean ... are you ... Oh christ, who's seeing Jackie? I mean is Paul in Jackie's picture?"

"Yah. Paul's around. Dating Jackie, I guess you could say. We work together, Paul and me. I take it Jackie didn't mention I was coming. See, Paul couldn't make it. And I was just leaving work. And Jackie said, why didn't I come for dinner then."

"So you're not ... "

"With Jackie? No. I think she was playing a little joke on you or something. But she said she had nice friends. So ... "

"So, here you are. And I'm very glad. To meet you. To have you. Here, I mean." I'm feeling flustered, feathered, befuddled. "I think we need another toast, Marvin. To an optimistic number. To the number six."

"Sure. February sixth. Here's to today."

We touch glasses but there's a definite hesitation, equation, energy. I brush my hand against Marvin's, then hold it there mesmerized by the heat of it, the beauty of the two symmetrical thumbs, the curl of the fingers, the hairs on the back of the dark hand. I'm drawn, melting closer. Marvin's leaning slightly toward me.

The table is littered with dirty napkins, an empty wine bottle. The radio's still on, FM in the background. Our two chairs are almost facing.

"Well, everyone's gone. Except you, Marvin."

"You seemed to want me to stay."

"I seem to … " And there they are, the lips. On mine. This seamless, endless, lip-lock. Six left digits hotly on my right thigh, think-I'm-gonna-die kind of thrill. I am so easy in a complicated, justifiable kind of way. I mean really. Who is this guy? Who cares? Take this opportunity. A tongue's a tongue, right. But this is a slow tongue, a lingering tongue. My mouth is remembering how to share its space, hopeful, open, more. If I pull away will it remember how to speak? I've got to know. I can't stay on this chair forever. And I can't possibly stand up and neck and … that's just physically difficult. I'll fall over or something. If he moves that fabulous hand up under my shirt … oh, man, here it comes …

"I have to lie down." I say into his lovely neck, his striped cotton shirt.

Now he pulls away, concerned. "Are you okay?"

"No. Yes. I'm fine. But I want to get comfortable, lie down. Come with me."

"To bed?"

"Yah." And although it's me saying it, stating it unquestionably, it can still be interpreted as a question, an out, an open door to a February night for Marvin. He doesn't make a run for it.

"Come on." And I get up, grab my cane (hardly sexy) and move my body (don't let me down now). Just make it to the bedroom. And I do. I make it. And Marvin's behind me.

"The cane, it's pretty sexy," he says.

"You think?" I'd give him a smile, but I have to concentrate, keep my eyes on the prize, the boudoir noir, the bed.

I sit on the edge feeling edgy but I can't stop it now, pass him the lighter. Can you light the candles?" I point to the pair on the bedside table. "Just put the books on the floor."

And there he is beside me, undoing my buttons with his magic hand, the thumbs work as an agile team. I can't use up all six orgasms in one night. Six. Six. Counting sixes. I'm going to have to slow down. Just one, got to make it good, just one. How long can I stay on the periphery, perimeter, primal brink? Our clothes keep coming off, dropping. There's a lot of skin, warm, smooth, tasty. Thumbs everywhere, on my breasts, chest, hair, and finally, down there, hot lips, clit lit and he's hard, too. We just kind of crawl in and here we are, lips and hands, torsos and digits, together under my flowered sheet, quilts. How could I have forgotten this kind of heat? My gawd, I'm gonna do it. I feel like a perpetual virgin, wonder if I'll bleed.

"Geez, have you got a condom?" I have to ask, don't I?

"For my thumb?"

"No. I want everything."

"My thumbs are everything. They're my tool, my organ, the real me."

"But ... you have a ... penis." I saw it, felt it against my leg, handled it. I reach down his belly to check. Yup, it's there all right.

"The thumb. Thumbs. It's the best way for me. Maybe for you, too."

I'm not averse to this new idea but really want the slide, body to body, the most skin to skin. No skimming.

"I want to come to Climax with you," says Marvin.

"Okay, the thumbs it is. But stay close. I want your body. Do they spill anything? Ejaculate anything?" That's not a sexy question. "Lips. I want your lips."

Breathing hard, moving slow, still that rocking motion. "Slower ... slower. What?"

"Climax. No spillage."

"Almost ... Almost there. Wait, make it last. I don't want it to be over yet." Hang on. Six minutes, six digits.

"No. I want to come with you ... to Climax."

"Okay, okay ... okay almost."

"Saskatchewan."

"Wait. Wait a sec ... Marvin, wait. Hold it." I have this terrible realization. An orgasmic mountain of doubt. When was Dr. Sharni's study done? And when was the last time I had an orgasm? After the study? After the study! Uh-oh. Melanie, we have a problem.

"Marvin, stop. Stop moving."

Marvin groans. "What? What's the matter? Now?"

I slide away from him, lifting the arm, the sixy sexy hand away. It still looks so damn good. But I just figured something out: This is all wrong. Wasn't meant to be at all. How could I be so stupid? I wasn't paying attention. Messed around with karmic magic.

"Hey, come back here." Marvin is reaching for me.

"I just realized I used up my number six before Christmas." I can't reveal everything to Marvin. He's a stranger, for gawd sake. And he's looking pretty spooked, getting nervous.

"What are you talking about? Do you want me to leave? Are you into numerology or something?" I can sense he wants to get up, make a run for it, but I'm sitting in the way.

"Sort of. It's complicated. I've been asking the universe for the wrong number. I need a five." I'm trying to buy time, control my mind, draw the line. Six. Six. Six. I keep looking at Marvin's hand poised on the sheet near my thigh, but not quite touching me. No contact zone with the six digits.

But Marvin is a genius. He lies back, lifts his arm a little and spreads out the thumb and fingers on his other hand ... all five. He raises an eyebrow.

"Marvin, that's it. Five. Say it for me, Marvin. Five." And he complies.

"Say it again for me. Come on. Humour me." And he does until I'm back under the covers, sinking into mouth-to-mouth. Sink. *Cinque.* Sunk.

Cougar Sighting, Siting, Citing

Charlene and I sit face to face at a sandwich shop in Saskatoon. She's flown in from Calgary to put on one of her psychic workshops. I've just driven into the city from Climax (my one-week temporary home) to touch base with her. The drive time was better than tolerable, only an hour, and the pale April sun had melted much of the snow. Winter was receding, even here.

We get busy reinforcing each other's confidence and our long-distance friendship. She's looking spiff, hair done up, a classy clairvoyant in a pastel-softened power suit, with a pendant of polished crystal at her throat to keep her grounded.

The waitress arrives with Charlene's veggie wrap, her wheatgrass soy smoothie, and my gamey venison burger, a recent craving. She takes a couple of thick soy sips, pointing out the benefits. "It keeps my skin youthful and glowing."

"Is that your secret, Char? I'll have to try it—some other time. You are looking fabulous. The workshop-lecture circuit's a good thing, I'm thinking."

"It's been quite a year. I've finally found my life path. You know, Mel, there are a lot of people out there who are ready to embrace the universal energy flow. What about you? "

"I'm good, great actually."

"Maybe your energy's good but not the walking, I noticed." She refuses to move her gaze from mine. My friends, the ethereal Charlene included, have a way of bringing me down to earth, sometimes a harder landing than the physical falling. Walking, never mind all else, has become my helter-skelter symbology, my diminishing icon, my infliction of reality.

"Don't remind me—another challenge—but I'm happy doing this. The writing. It's good for me. Sitting is what I do best and a change of scenery is invigorating." I don't tell Charlene what I'm thinking, which is a friendly "screw off!"

"Yah, but Saskatchewan? Climax?"

"Hey, don't knock it. Stubble can be sexy. Anyway, it's just a hiccup on the journey. A brief retreat."

"So there's someone here with sexy stubble?"

"No, I mean the natural surroundings. I'm a prairie girl, anyway, you know—deep roots. Speaking of deep, the Tarot reading you did for me in February, it was pretty amazing." I add on a quick tag, "Not that I should be surprised."

"Maybe, you've just been more open, Mel," says Charlene, ready to defend.

"Well, whatever it is ... was ... I had a good feeling about that near future, which is now," I say to my friend Charlene, my medium, my palm reader Tarot-carder tea-leaf reader. "I knew it when you said it, that it would happen. Do you remember? The man, the wheat colour or pale sand or something sun-lit or whatever it was that you saw me travelling through and then the schooling being *big*?"

"Sure. Of course. And it was all good and important," Charlene says, agreeing, expanding, expounding. "Your cat shakra will empower you but you have to talk to the universe about what you need. Ask the great universe *for* it."

"And I did. I do. But listen. You said there'd be a man. You said he'd be younger. You said he wanted my mind." And want was right at the top of my list, all right, just more to do with my own body connection. "So, off I went to Climax, and there he was. Not even a stranger, really. But surrounded by wheat fields and driving an old Jaguar, the colour of sand. You said I'd be driving through sand or blonde or something like that." I notice two men sitting down at the counter. "Hey, when did glasses become sexy, anyway? I never noticed that before."

"So, this guy's got glasses. Tall? Short?"

"I've suddenly started to notice them on everyone."

"Well, you wear them, now, for reading, don't you?"

"Yah, don't remind me. But I like them on other people, on men. Strange. But anyway, he's not as tall as I expected."

"Expected? You are exuding positivism."

"He's not much taller than me. And he's younger than you said he'd be. Maybe late twenties."

"Jesus, Mel, that'll take some energy."

"Well, not really. I mean it's not realistic to actually think it will go anywhere but he's funny, smart, exciting … I mean, just in the desire department."

"Really?" Charlene raises one eyebrow into an exaggerated crescent.

"Kind of a pleasurable spark. You know what I mean—the possibilities of attraction. You forget what it feels like, even if it is one-sided. Ah, I'm just rolling it around in my head." My body is the thing I have to worry about. Hot and bothered body. Not even insightful Charlene can foresee the serious nature of this quest. I can't let on either about the orgasms running out. She would see me as desperate. I couldn't stand that.

"How long have you been in Climax now?"

The week's almost done. I leave for the coast in a couple of days. Long drive."

"Me, too. I'll fly back day after tomorrow, after this workshop." Charlene adds with foreboding, "Back to the rain. Hey, what about the writing? You haven't mentioned what it is you're working on. Isn't that what you're here for?"

"Oh, the retreat's been great. It's such an inspiration. Not just the writing itself, although my project's coming along. My collection, the poetry is driving me, not the novel right now." Where do I come up with these things? I'm not even a player, only literally playing. "But the people doing the writing are amazing. All over the board. Fascinating stuff."

"Poetry now, eh? It's not my thing. So, is that where you met this guy?"

"Well, yah, but I actually sort of knew him before."

"How well?" she says, smirking.

"No, Charlene, nothing like that. He did a weekend workshop, a writing workshop a couple of years ago in Penticton." He was attractive, all right, but every woman in the class wanted to chat him up, impress him, undress him, something. Anyway, the line-up was not only too long to get through, it was a time in my life I wasn't interested in that time-consuming lust stuff. I wasn't interesting then either. I wasn't potentially sexual. Libidinous. Circumstances have changed. I'm down to four big Os.

"Oh," says Charlene who's apparently reading part of my mind. Then she slips into small talk, really small, which is unusual for her. But I'm thankful. I keep nodding, half-listening, but really I'm thinking back to my first class at the retreat in Climax. An orientation actually, but it was the first in-depth step into the creative process on the prairie page, and right into a self-revelation of my desire. Which is what Charlene seems to be prattling on about. Attractions. And that's the beauty. Right there. The memory, the feeling of attraction, wanting to attract, allure, stir somebody. Ignite a small fire.

So I fake conversational continuity. "Yah, I know. It's crazy. These things. But listen. I only have an attraction like this about every ten years."

Charlene says, "You've got to be kidding. I thought you had one every five minutes. You're always hot."

"No. No, I'm not. Really. Just lately. There was a cop. About ten years ago. Nothing happened. Nothing ever happens. It's the desire that keeps me going. Makes me want to shave my legs, paint my toenails, buy a new bra, maybe even a black one."

"That's one crazy path to choose, Mel. Bizarre. You can't survive on desire."

"Yah, well, watch me. It's a different kind of high. For a while at least." I don't really believe it either, but acknowledging desire in the face of possible failure is empowering in itself.

"This young guy ... aren't you kind of preying?"

"Absolutely, I'm praying. Down on my knees every night." Is Charlene prying? "Just kidding. I'm asking the universe daily, just like you told me to."

"No, I mean preying as in predatory."

"Maybe I am preying, just a little."

"You're whacked. I still love you but you're weirding me out. I have to go to the ladies. I'll be back. Grab the bill, will you?"

"Sure, go ahead," I say, watching her go. She's always well-groomed. Makes me feel unsophisticated. Unkempt. Wild. Feral. An un-so-phist-i-cat.

But the desire idea keeps feeding my imagination. I can put myself back in that first class. Genres, he was talking about. Genre language. Lingual gender, I think. The words slid off his tongue. Slid off Jack's tongue. And his example, first thing, was want ads in newspapers. I could hardly sit still. Why did I pick the front row, the closest, almost face to face? Was I on a self-propelled collision course? Subconsciously looking for the impact of collusion, through the writing, of course (in the course). We were looking through the classifieds for obvious categories—to buy, to rent, obituaries, appliances.

The trouble started with a look at car ads, their language loaded with sexual innuendo—sporty, sexy, sleek, spoilers, side skirts, blue metallic body, performance package, heated leather seats, spokes. I took notes: panther leather seats, a '69 Mercury Cougar. The discussion went on about commodity language as one expression of the world and its target audience, the language becoming its own entity, no less bizarre than its human scribes. And fit was absolutely on my mind. Lay-a-lip-lock-on-me-baby kind of fit. The innocence (or was it?) of those syllabically minimal ad words sliding off a particular tongue, past sensual lips, the unprotected projection, the sonic sensuality.

My hairline beads perspiration just thinking about it. Imagining bodily contact. Becoming a cat act. Feline language. Even I could learn to purr.

I call the waitress over. "Do you have beer on tap?"

"No, but we have canned."

"That'll do. Just one of those."

"All we have is Wildcat."

"But, of course. Sounds, well, just right. Perfect. Uh, then, can I get the bill? Thanks."

She nods. "One Cat coming up."

"You bet."

Takes me back to sweating in that classroom. Fifteen of us, a typical mix, two men, thirteen women (mostly my age), two other smokers (thank gawd!). The heat. No one else seemed warm at all. A couple of women still wore jackets.

I have to quit this. I pick up the newspaper from the empty table behind me, flip through it. Charlene must be putting on her karmic face. And there on page four, I'm slapped, slammed, struck by this headline: "Cougars and You: A Safety Guide." I'm praying, preying for this guy's unsafety. I want to be a threat, put him in just a little danger. I'm feeling pretty carnivorous.

Charlene approaches the table. "You might need this," she says, smirking, tossing a condom, Lynx brand, onto the open newspaper. I close it quickly, covering up the suggestive evidence, hers and mine.

"Don't be too good," she says, and we both laugh. We share a goodbye hug, wish each other well, and she's gone. Maybe, just maybe, she's more psychically perceptive than I give her credit for.

I sip my Wildcat, turn back to page four, slip the Lynx into my purse. The species is close enough in my books. I hadn't realized there was a cougar population in Saskatchewan. I'll have to read between the lines.

COUGARS AND YOU: A SAFETY GUIDE

1. COUGARS ARE MOST ACTIVE AT DUSK AND DAWN. THEY WILL, HOWEVER, ROAM AND HUNT AT ANY TIME OF THE DAY AND NIGHT AND IN ALL SEASONS.

> Right. I can really only pull off this intimacy thing under cover of night. The failure of the body is always magnified by day.

2. GENERALLY, COUGARS ARE SOLITARY.

> That is so me, most of the time anyway. I'll make sure to leave my other classmates behind.

3. CONSIDER GETTING A DOG. KEEP A RADIO PLAYING. IF THERE HAVE BEEN SIGHTINGS, TAKE AN ESCORT. DON'T WALK ALONE.

> Okay, I'll be the escort, won't let him walk alone. If he's got a dog, I'll have biscuits in my pocket, just in case. And the radio's just silly. Who writes this stuff?

4. NEVER APPROACH A COUGAR. ALTHOUGH THEY NORMALLY AVOID CONFRONTATION, ALL COUGARS ARE UNPREDICTABLE.

> I'll do the approaching. I'm never interested in a confrontation, although unpredictability has its attractions. I am so there.

5. STAY CALM. TALK TO THE COUGAR IN A CONFIDENT MANNER.

> Confidence, he's got. I'll just have to keep him on the edge with me. Just enough. Not too much. Liquor always helps amp up the action.

6. RAPID MOVEMENT MAY PROVOKE AN ATTACK. DO NOT RUN. I REPEAT, DO NOT RUN. TRY TO BACK AWAY FROM THE COUGAR SLOWLY. OTHERWISE, INSTINCTIVE ATTACK MAY BE THE RESULT.

> I'll make sure we stay face to face until it's too late for him to make a break for it. Hold him with my eyes. Lying won't be necessary. Instinct rules—basic, primal, absolutely yes.

7. DO ALL YOU CAN TO ENLARGE YOUR IMAGE. DON'T CROUCH DOWN OR TRY TO HIDE. PICK UP STICKS OR BRANCHES AND WAVE THEM AROUND.

> I'll stroke his ego, make him big, make him hard, won't let him hide. I can wave around chopsticks, cocktail skewers, toothpicks even.

8. COUGARS ARE A VITAL PART OF OUR DIVERSE WILDLIFE. SEEING A COUGAR SHOULD BE AN EXCITING AND REWARDING EXPERIENCE, WITH BOTH YOU AND THE COUGAR COMING AWAY UNHARMED.

> This is absolute gospel—the vitality, life force, compulsion, desire, excitement, and rewards on all sides. Charmed but unharmed. No alarms, bells or whistles until after. Just straight-up heat exchange.

I wait until the last class to make my move. I like to raise the stakes. Push the possibility of failure, in, well, anything, to make the success pot a little sweeter. That way I only have myself to royally blame for a short time. Plus it leaves me lots of time to change my mind in the meantime, chicken out.

But not this time. Someone has brought a bottle of wine to the classroom, paper cups too, just for a quick farewell toast. A small buzz. A touch of courage. A little added heat brings desire to the fore. I really can't concentrate on anything else, not even the writing.

Spirits are high. Everyone's ready to head home, which is mostly right here on the prairies, two farther east. I'll be heading all the way to the coast. One other woman, Yvonne, the youngest in the group, is returning to Nelson.

I sidle around the hugs when it's over, prolong the book-bag shuffle until they're all finally gone except Jack, who suddenly looks beat. My time has come. To either speak or wave goodbye.

"I'll miss this. We're all on our own again with the writing."

Jack's maintaining his professionalism.

"I kind of hate to go back to my room," I say. "Are you up for the pub? I'll buy you a thank-you drink." It's out of my hands now, up to the universe.

"I won't be very good company. These workshops are pretty draining." Then seeing my disappointment, he softens his resolve. "Ah, sure. What the hell. One drink won't hurt. We can walk from here."

"Uh, the walking's not so good."

"Sorry. Right."

This is okay, I think. Let him feel a little awkward for a change. I can afford to be generous here. "It's okay. You can ride with me. Unless you want the walk."

"No, no. Let's go."

So we do. It's a short drive. The parking lot's empty. The farmers are all at home in bed, dreaming about crop-seeding and a good season. The pub looks out over absolutely nothing. I checked this out earlier. No distractions. Except when we walk in there are two other women from the class, which kind of throws me. So we pretty much have to sit there with them. No way around it. I play it cool on the outside. The inside, on the other hand, is really cooking. These other women are threatening my territory. They're revealing a little too much in the personal department, one with a penchant for intellectual men, the other with a sexually dysfunctional husband. I refuse to play catch-up. Jack, on the other hand, reveals only tidbits.

He's playing it close to his chest. That's right, I think, breast your cards, baby. I'm in for the long haul as far as evenings go. I can just outlast them. And I do. They finally wobble out.

I'm getting a little slurry myself. Jack's forgotten his one drink rule. We're warming up, but I'm not getting a very clear reading on him. Not clear at all. Figure I'll just quit messing around. It's almost closing time.

"So, attractive man, how about it?" I ask. "Just sex, right now."

"What?"

"I said, sex ..."

"I got that part." He stares at the clock behind the bar.

Is this awkward or what? Impulse can be a bad thing.

He finally speaks. "I'll be right back. Hold that thought." As if I could do anything but. He heads to the washroom. Maybe he's considering. I order more drinks.

"I should really go," he says, but sits down again, eyeing the last round. Aha, he's got a weakness.

"It's okay, not to worry. We all head back to our real lives tomorrow."

"Yah," he says, all thoughtful, but he's smiling. There's a long silence. We sip away the minutes.

"My turn," I say, motioning to the washroom. "Be right back." I do my un-svelte cane-leaning drag-stagger-walk to the door that says Gals instead of Ladies. I'm thanking the universe, prematurely it turns out. The zipper on my pants is stuck. Really, really stuck and that MS-urgency trigger of the toilet is getting beyond uncomfortable. In fact, I'm leaking. I weigh my options. None. I clutch and yank and finally just sit down on the damn porcelain. The leak accelerates to a full-blown flood. My jeans darken. My socks dampen. All of three drops actually hit the toilet. And then I sit there because I cannot for the life of me think what to do. So I sit away the minutes now, alone.

The waitress comes in and talks to me through the cubicle door.

"Are you okay, Sugar?" she asks. "Your friend was worried about you."

"I have a dilemma."

"Uh, is there something I can do?"

"Indeed, there is," I say, as I dig in my purse, which now also has a soggy bottom. I explain the situation to her in detail, and then pass a hundred bucks under the cubicle to pay the bill and to sweeten the pie of my new accomplice as she hides my car round back, tells Jack I must have left, then retrieves my back-up wheelchair for me when he's gone. Long gone. Funny how desire goes out the window in the face of flooding. Wish I had an ark, except I wouldn't fit in. No flawed creatures allowed, and every animal has a partner. Even the cougar.

I'm looking forward to the drive home alone across that stretch of prairie, then the lift of highway through the foothills, up and over to the coastal side and back to my other life. I'm leaving town nice and early with a bagel and a mega-cup of Timmy's by my side, all eager to put distance between me and last night. There's somebody up ahead—with a thumb out. I don't pick up hitchhikers anymore. I feign road concentration, grab a quick glance. Mistake, mistake.

It's bloody Yvonne, my classmate, holding a sad illegible cardboard sign and looking more like fifteen than twenty-five. Long blonde braids, a bright toque. I keep going. I'll never see her again.

It takes me a couple of minutes to break my rule, brake the van, and reverse through the potholes until we're face to face through the passenger window. She's really glad to see me, she says as she climbs in, stowing a backpack and a case of pale ale at her feet. She missed the bus, the bus to Nelson, which is not just hours but days away. I offer to get her to a town where she can catch another bus. She looks wet-eyed like a thankful puppy. So I offer to get her all the way there. She bursts into grateful tears. So I stop thinking of things to offer her except a cooler to park the beer in, not that I'm interested in liquor today. Yvonne is effusive.

"This is so *so* great of you, Mel. Like fate or destiny. You just showing up like that. Honestly, the bus trip is hell anyway. This is just so *so* much better."

"No kidding."

"You know I can drive if you get tired. And I've got a little gas money. I can get my ticket reimbursed."

"Yeah, sure. Let's just get moving. I'm ready to go home."

Then she just talks. A lot.

I draw the line at writing. Nix anything Climax-related due to the fact that I'm philosophically wrung-out. To tell her I'm physically and emotionally hungover would give her the upper hand. I'm more of a sick kitten than a cougar today, and it's going to be one helluva long drive.

But maybe, just maybe, this drive with Yvonne will take my mind off failures. Bodily, bawdily. Don't even think about it. That's dangerous territory, a post-erogenous zone: vanity, insanity, disability all rolled into one messy night. I need to be sexless. It's safer.

Yvonne buckles up as we head for the Trans-Canada. Then due west. We drive, chat, stop for gas, then a rest-stop lunch, buns and cheese, one juicy tomato, sliced, out of the cooler. I'm beat, still in recovery from humiliation and shooters, Red-headed Sluts they were called, peach schnapps and Jagermeister. Herbal, my ass.

"Want me to drive for a bit?" Maybe she's another freakin' mind reader—like Nadine—with a third eye, and I'm blind.

"You know, that would be great. I might just shut my eyes for an hour."

She takes over, adjusts the seat, puts on her Bono shades, tunes the radio to a clear station playing the Eagles. It's "Life in the Fast Lane," and that's right where we are. She's comfortable with the van in moments. My eyelids are so heavy, speech dull. I tilt the seat back as far as it will go—which isn't far—and drift into three-dimensional sleep. Only in the afternoon do these dreams arrive at my subconscious doorstep. No matter where I am, sleep in these particular daylight hours gives me memorable hallucinations, clear visions.

I'm not disappointed. The radio plays on. We take the corners gently, smooth curves bend my mind to scenes, forgiving, familiar, then tender. I sleep with a degree of rhyme, shameless.

> I dreamt of this man, pretty sweet, long
> sleeved, (*con coeur*) smile, lying
> with his head glassed in my afternoon
> lap, his neck curved, collar turned
> to my thigh, couched
> in a sparse lobby.
>
> There was nothing luxuri
> yes but the warmth of his chest
> under my resting palm, leaves
> splayed—fan turning
> above his open laptop
> on the tiles.
>
> This was later, after my stroll through
> the wrong apartment, high wind
> owed, video-dead. A tailored stranger there
> under a fedora, blonde locks, *oro*,

met me at the open door
but didn't question (concur), switched on the fans,
gestured to the stares heading down.

This was later, after finding my key
board faded out, letters erased, digitals under
dressed, smooth finger pads, couldn't get my mess
age across, blue caller me.
I'd have to (conquer) walk.

I feel the car braking hard, hear Yvonne cursing. My eyes pop open in alarm and there's this bright angel winging straight at us. Well, okay, a hang-glider, with a wingspan looking to be almost as wide as the road and he's coming straight at us, flying, wobbling, floating earthward. His long black hair blows back—a dark angel.

Jesus! He tips to the right and his wing skitters across the windshield, a lime-green nylon whoosh and clatter, the snap of the radio antenna. Yvonne's slammed the brakes on all the way now. The green wings tumble over and behind us landing in a shallow ditch. Christ!

"Gawd, did we kill him?" she says, and I mumble my uncertainty, trying to look through the back window where a narrow strip of green nylon flutters.

"No, look," she says. "He's moving—I think."

She gets out and runs back. I shuffle over to the driver's seat and reverse for the second time today to get a read on the situation without leaving the vehicle.

The guy untangles himself from his wings with some help from Yvonne. He's a lot less ethereal without them—a short, stocky leather-clad not-so-young guy with long wavy locks and a nasty cut on his rugged forehead. An overgrown beard, heavy moustache, and a foul stream of French and English curses. He assumes I was driving.

"You hit me!" he accuses.

"His name is Yvon," Yvonne volunteers.
"Are you all right?" I ask.
"For real," says Girl-Yvonne, groovin' on destiny. "So *so* cool, eh?"
"You hit me?!"
"I'm pretty sure you hit us. You don't look all right." I offer my first-aid kit through the window to Girl-Yvonne. It's the least I can do.

It takes a good hour, not to bandage his minor gash but to make a plan and put it into action. First, to fold his slightly tattered wings and lash them to the roof. No easy feat. Those wings stretch from the nose to well past the rear. We look more like an oversized exotic insect than anything from heaven. Second, to rearrange stuff in the van and settle him into the rear seat. I dispense Tylenol for his increasing headache. Lots of Tylenol. For me too cuz I feel the hint of a lawsuit coming on. Third, to calm everybody down. And, fourth, to drive! Anywhere. Fast. Preferably somewhere with a bathroom. And food. It'll be me behind the wheel because Girl-Yvonne is already dispensing beer.

It's only 6:00 but it's getting dark cuz it's only April, so now I really would like to see a lit-up Travelodge sign with a comfy bed. As soon as we drop off Boy-Yvon, who says he's from Bigstick Lake (well behind us) and he'd really like to make it to Taboo Creek but he'll settle for Breastwork Hill, which sends Girl-Yvonne into hysterics and me into yawns. But the conversation's better than nothing and the radio's out of commission. He's a walking storybook and his bizarre method of travel—getting up to speed atop semis before catapulting his winged self into the sky—is a lifestyle not a hobby. This doesn't even faze me. Since Marvin, I have to admit there's a lot I don't know or understand. Or need to believe.

We don't have enough gas to make it to Breastwork Hill, so we pull in at a truck-stop motel with a congregation of big rigs, every colour and style. A lot of them are really flashy with dingleballs up the yin yang. The motel, surrounded by oil-drenched pavement and chuffing engines and motors and reefers, is not inviting or particularly clean. There's only one room left. With one double bed. I have a bad feeling about this. When we get to the room, the key won't work, so Girl-Yvonne gives it a boot. The door opens but the couple already lying in our one double bed aren't exactly happy to meet us. Another mistake. This gives me a worse feeling. Boy-Yvon slips away, and I'm kinda pissed about that.

Girl-Yvonne circles the winged van while I lean on it and smoke and contemplate sleeping in it as the only option—an undesirable one. My leg'll seize up, get all spastically uncooperative, refusing to bend or unbend. And my foot'll swell. I should elevate my leg right now, in fact, because extended sitting does the same thing. I'm just getting ready to tuck myself into my seat. There's no way I'm going to brush my teeth or anything else in the pizza joint. Girl-Yvonne's trying to be sweet because she partly blames herself for the situation. I'm just cranky because I partly blame her too, and the real perpetrator has deserted us. I'm cussing him out under my breath when he strides across the lot with a wink and a cherubic smile.

Boy-Yvon, it turns out, has tracked down one of his trucker-buddies, who's having a little sleepover with another trucker-buddy, and he's managed to wrangle us a bunk. I could care less how he got it or what he calls it. And it's no bunk. It's a full-on luxury sleeper, right behind the cab of a cherry Peterbilt. I need a lot of help to get up the shiny chrome ladder into the thing but it's worth it. All fancy-shmancy. Studded red leather. Clean sheets in a drawer. And a bathroom!

Over pizza and beer in our crimson abode we get a little comfier, have a few laughs, kick back. Girl-Yvonne's giggling and snorting at some joke I didn't get, when she starts to cough. That red-faced teary-eyed coughing where you can't stop and it goes on and on. And then it doesn't. And her face gets redder. And she's kind of beating at her chest. I don't get it at first, like the joke I missed. Boy-Yvon gets it. He pulls her up and leaps behind her grasping her around the belly. Now I get it. He's thrusting his fist up just below her ribcage like he knows what he's doing, and I guess he does because Girl-Yvonne coughs out a chunk of pepperoni. She's okay. The funny thing is Boy-Yvon's still fooling around and keeps thrusting but not with his fist, just his body. And Girl-Yvonne's giggling again. Oh my! It's a good thing I'm no longer interested in sex. I'm not. Really.

    I start to like Boy-Yvon because he doesn't like me back. And he saved the day. Plus, I think the semi-simultaneous calamity and close-call syndrome has drawn my companions together without me. They seem to have their own little something-something going on, so I don't have to get involved. We're all really relieved and kind of euphoric about Boy-Yvon's safe landing and Girl-Yvonne's semi-choking episode and a coolly unusual place to sleep and decent pizza and cold beer. And we don't have to drive so we have a little toke too—hotboxing in compact luxury. The Yvon(ne)s take off for a walk (so they say) and I cuddle myself trying to get all cozy and drift off. And wake up chilly. And drift off, feeling slightly less worn out and a little more left out and wishing my name was fronted with a Y too, like a pair of tightie-whities.

    I hear them come back. And I can see them all giggly and flirty and kissy. And then the light's out and Yvonne pounces on me all playful and climbs over me and both Yvon(ne)s burrow in. On either side of me. Brrr. Cuddle. Okay. Tickle. Not exactly okay. But I can't help but laugh. And I can feel them laughing too. Or more to the point, they're kinda feeling me feeling them laugh. I'm the "feeling" in the funny "sandweech." Boy-Yvon's like a thick coarse rye, Girl-Yvonne's like Wonderbread. We start singing, *Sandwiches are beautiful. Sandwiches are fine* by that Penner guy. I figure they'll quit tickle-touching. That doesn't happen.

I say in the dark, "Come on, you guys, really," but I guess that could be interpreted in multiple ways. By multiple minds attached to multiple lips and fingers. Before you know it we're all rolled up in a kitten-ball laughing and kissing and purring and kissing and murmuring and kissing. And being in the middle of tickling and kissing is a pretty sweet spot to be in. And then it doesn't matter anymore who's in the middle. Or who's doing what, but I can definitely tell the difference between unmanscaped hairy-everywhere Guy-rye and Girl-wonder, who has her own coiffed landing strip down south, which makes me wonder if that's what initially drew the hang-glider to the van. Regardless, I have no complaints about either. Touchy-feely head-to-toe.

I'm feeling really generous. Downright selfless. It doesn't even bother me that both Yvon(ne)s climax at least once and that I've had a hand (not to blatantly mention other parts) in making that happen. And I don't mind staying on this drifting pleasure-plateau for a good long time until sleep takes over. We're winding down one by one. Boy-Yvon fades first but we're all still cuddled up. Oh. Did I say plateau? There seems to be a change in topographical altitude. Maybe Girl-Yvonne's the real angel. My oh my. Here it comes. Ohhh. Sweeeeet. Myyyyyy. And keeps coming. It's not one of those intense pangy clenching orgasms but more an extended rippling circling wave of deliciousness.

Mmmmmmm ...

... mmmmmm ...

... mmmmm ...

mmmm ...

mmm ...

mm ...

m ...

m

Maybe this whole trio scenario is so *so* good (as Girl-Yvonne would say) because it was unplanned, unexpected, and sort of has a last-day-on-earth feeling. A long, long day. One I won't forget. Until I try to. In the awkward morning, when cougars and kittens, angels and arks head back to the shadows.

Kim Clark

Dar-Win-or-Lose-ling Techno Love

I have to do something. Now. Maybe I should try online dating. I mean it's been months since Climax, a whole West Coast summer gone. I stopped writing, even sometimes stopped bathing. The humid heat slowed my motion down to a barely upright crawl and the haze of Prozac, then Zoloft, even Celexa left me feeling like I was missing a whole lot of something, just not sex. Selective, yes. Inhibitor, yes. But I've only been half here, and not necessarily the good half. Peace and calm are synonymous with half-dead. Without desire, there's a gaping hole in my supposedly happy self. Artificial serotonin, be damned. I need a boost of the real thing. It's not like I'm depressed, but more that my friends keep telling me, convincing me almost, that I must be depressed. "That's the problem," they say, all self-satisfied with their diagnosis.

Cold-turkeying the pills has its up and down side, too. The up is Heightened Olfactory Raunchy Nasty Yearning (acronym HORNY) and the down is the same cuz pretty soon I won't have a way out of it. Nothing left but that Fleshly Retrogressive Idiosyncratic Genital Id Destimulation (acronym FRIGID). Satisfaction, a thing of the almost past.

Even if there was actually someone out there to do this last (almost) dirty-sweet deed, I'd have to find a way to attract that particular person, and, no, this cannot be a mechanical self-induced fiasco. It's the attracting that's getting so much harder. Oh, don't think harder. Think more difficult, more challenging.

But, it's true. I cannot use those body parts, the ones that used to be annoyingly alluring, in any way that is not awkward. Fingers and hips and even the ass that wasn't half-bad, all seem to go off in odd directions. My body makes people nervous. Especially the younger ones. They can't trust it, and neither can I. They think they might have to take responsibility for me temporarily if I slip up or fall down. Trust me. I know. Attractions run the other way, and fast, at any sign of incapacity. Even little things like leg cramps or wet pants have a dampening effect on a potentially passionate moment. Oh, don't think passionate!

And while the wheelchair is an attraction in its own odd way, it's not, believe me, a sexual one. If that was all it took, I'd be parked in it right now. But the chair kind of demands its own set of rules. Like another person, on any kind of hill or slant or in a doorway, but then I become invisible if I'm with my pusher, and I don't mean drugs here. I mean cousin, friend, volunteer. In the big sociocultural scheme of things, the general consensus is wheelchair (substitute any disability) equals nonsexual. What happened to the notion of enhanced senses that's supposed to accompany disability limitations? It's a pretty cool idea but I'm still waiting for the special delivery package with mine in it. I mean we all know the biggest organ, skin, is as sweet as it is useful, holding in all those circling bodily fluids, right? But how did I overlook that for so long? Even avoided it. Refuted it.

Maybe I could just call up Marvin, or the Yvon(ne)s or the cowboy from twenty-some years ago who was so fantastically acrobatic from hanging off the saddle and doing his special trick-roping thing. There was certainly something to be said for living in motels called the Flamingo or Saratoga or Western Star. Who knew that was as good as it would get? I had an old friend offer to help me out of this pinch, but really, a childhood friend? That would be incestuous or something, I told him.

I need a freakin' fearless lion tamer or an astronaut. No, too spacey. An all-star wrestler or a dominatrix or a ballerina or a pool boy. But you have to move in the right circles to meet these folks. You might even need a little money. My assets are shrinking as we speak. Pretty thin pockets. Pretty slim options.

I've been paying people, a small fortune in fact, to touch me for years so I wouldn't have to waste my time on desire or seduction or the noose of a failing relationship. I'm not alone, here. You're with me on this. Relate. There is spa pampering, facials, cranial sacral treatments, even the cracking chiropractic sessions or the fluttering almost-touch of healing hands.

The shampoos and root stimulation at the local hair salon were the cat's meow until they changed the name of the place to Curl Up 'n Dye. That finished the pleasure for me.

Then the massages by masseur practitioner Bob were pretty sweet, until the fee went up and the government subsidies went down. Maybe he had a genetic connection to Marvin and his magic thumbs. But Bob was just a muscle pleasure man. Don't say muscle! Don't think pleasure!

Tanya, the pedicure queen, could have sent me off to pedia-heaven if I'd been so inclined but no dice back then. Who knew the truth about desperation when you had all your senses? Sensibilities? All your functions?

Dr. Sounomono was the small but powerful pleasure/pain man. Acupuncture ruled until he introduced me to Major Moxi. Forget those cool slender needles, even with the electric current enhancers. Heat, moxibustion, made the body sing, the legs bend and zing into taut bows. Small burnings of coned herb on those precise pressure points gave me so much more moxie, and such a damn huge hit of relief just to walk out of his door. I got a bit of a lift from the smoky smell on my skin on the drive home, too, the small precise blisters some kind of proof of escaping toxins, bad chi, bad general attitude.

The most amazing thing about all these professional sessions, especially with Bob the Masseur, was that my totally illegible handwriting improved enough for me to write exquisitely penned cheques. Like nothing was impossible. The handwriting never lasted longer than the money, though. And if not healed physically by any of the above, at least I felt damn good afterwards.

The weird thing about my not-so-distant future is that while I crave touch and bodily contact (and please, please, please a few more big bangs) it may really come down to just that, the contact I mean, but with a whole lot of waiting in between. Spoon that soup into my mouth. Wait. Oh, don't think mouth. I do not want early-bird entry into the seniors' club, regardless of their welcoming me and anyone else with a cane or other mobility equipment. Even for discount Tuesdays.

Jackie's been on my case to take some kind of control of my life, find something meaningful to do with myself. Getting out from under this orgasmic numbers game would definitely be helpful.

The phone rings and it's Charlene, not Jackie as I expected.

"Mel," she says, "Are you at the computer?" How does she know this stuff? Am I floating around in her crystal ball or something?

"Hello to you too, Char. How's tricks?"

"Very funny. No tricks. But check this out. This month should be really hot for you."

I have to ask. "Is this a free reading?"

"Yes, Mel. It's free. Go to my website. Check out your horoscope. I know you think it's a waste of your precious time, but today's the beginning of something important for you, if you're open to it."

"Okay, okay. Thanks."

"Let me know how it goes, Mel."

"Char? Charlene?" But the line's dead and she's gone. I'll have a look. What harm can it do?

> This is a time of successful energetic activity. You may bring your affairs to a climax through intelligent planning and foresight, which are available to you under this influence if you make a conscious effort to take advantage of them.

A couple of words stand out so I mentally capitalize and underscore. <u>Successful</u> and <u>Climax</u>.

Dating just might be the answer. I will try the internet. No, I will succeed at it. I've avoided that whole scene. It just creeps me out, but maybe it's a good fit now for a misfit like me. I don't mean a badass who got caught but a misfit, someone naughty who didn't get caught. Until now. I mean physically as well as legally. This damn body is blackmailing me, I swear. I want to sue myself for not holding up my side of the bargain. If I won, I could afford to resume my pay-per-touch lifestyle.

I get my body, my self, set up at the computer. I have a new goal. A date, so to speak, or an über-hookup, or some cosmic connection. I have a tall Bacardi Coke at my side, a cigarette behind my ear to make me feel nonchalant, like a construction worker in those faded, torn, too tight jeans that I love to generically love. I crank up Nickelback for their pounding innuendo beat. Chad baby *still wants to be that someone that you're with*. So I'll Google, but before I even touch a key there are offers. No! I do not want a dinner date with Cindy Margolis. But Click to Enter sounds kind of erotic.

Okay, I admit Jackie might have been right about my general concentration problem, not that I'll admit that to her, but in this one area of interest (without synthetic drugs) it is unswerving, relentless. Sex.

So I peruse my options. There are 450 million sites for sex, 195 million sites for dating, 460,000 for lion tamer, 35,000 if you Google all three together.

The possibilities are endless, unlike my current sexual situation. I refuse to be overwhelmed and persevere with research. I want to pick the online dating site that's the right fit. I dig, click, and scroll. For three days. Forget the rum, this is serious business. Red Bull is the only answer. Ignore the phone, the weekly garbage pickup, even the warm sun, the cool evenings out there beyond my computer screen.

Six Degrees of Altered Sensation

It's easy to rule out a lot of these sites. I'm not into the Christian dating or Baha'i or Scientology find-a-spiritual-soulmate connections. I need something newer, fresher than friends-reuniting dating. I'm not too young for Cougar dating and it is Canuck style, but realistically I'm not hungry enough yet and I'm in too rough shape to be arm candy for Sugar-daddy dating. I'm not interested in my previous jockette status for athletic sports dating. But you can classify yourself as "spectator only" or even "team mascot," and you have the option to communicate with an armchair tennis aficionado or a retired pro footballer or an active hockey-pucker or someone into fishing, but the hooks get messy—maybe they fit more into the fetish-mate love sites.

I can't get on a motorcycle so Harley-dating is out, and liberalhearts, which claims to bring together like-minded democrats, Greens, and environmentalists, doesn't do it for me either. Neither does exclusive racial or ethnic dating. I mean, really, I'm a mongrel culturally open-armed Canadian. I've never been a nurse or a firefighter or a soldier, so uniform-dating is out, but there seem to be a lot of the same lookie loos poking around in there as on fetish love.

There is vegetarian, vegan and rawfoodist dating, but I like meat. There is dating for "thinking" people but I do too much of that already and would really prefer less affected brilliant conversation and a little more fruitful action.

Hey, here's an interesting one—radiocarbon dating. But I can't fit in there either. I'm not a traditional totem pole or an ancient fresco. But surprisingly, my MS disease shares two thirds of the AMS acronym for Accelerator Mass Spectrometry dating. And this facility guarantees the same kind of thing as all the other dating sites: excellent service, rapid turnaround time, liaison with submitters and confidentiality. The promise of accurate measurements, though, has me thinking. Does size matter when I have numbers to worry about?

I am suddenly feeling wretched looking at the latest site. Wretched enough to wash a few dishes, straighten the sheets on my empty bed, and notice the rising sweep of wind-tossed branches against a fierce sky. I turn up the heat, pluck my eyebrows, stand on the bathroom scale (almost fall off), then apply a whole tube of anti-wrinkle cream (everywhere). It's not just that I'm more than a titch over the thirty-five-year age limit of the Darwin-dating site. I've lived through my share of selfish, shallow vanity and all that arrogant youthful immortality. It's way creepier than that, even if it is a spoof, which it's not. I would never have been voted in even before the disability took hold. Although the Darwinesque site doesn't specify physical abnormalities in its list of entry denial criteria, applications get a big red X if you admit to having red hair, too many freckles, sags or rolls, too much body hair, pasty skin, etc. etc. etc. The list goes on, and I'm so out of there.

I'll go the regular route. Match-dot, or date-dot or plenty-of-fish-dot or charmony. I need to answer 300 questions about my personality, so I have a complete profile to match up by techno-chemistry. It claims to be scientific. But anytime profiling is mentioned I get jumpy and look over my shoulder for cops. And not only do I not want to see my profile on screen or in print, but I have to look at myself with some kind of honesty while marketing a desirable image. Plus I have to concentrate, stay on task, which is too much like a job in advertising. I can't help searching local areas, familiar locales, to see what kinds of people are listed. Sure enough, here's my lawyer and my first husband (so that's what he looks like now), and the neighbourhood postal clerk.

I fill out the form to the best of my ability, lying only a little about my age. Failing to mention the fact that I have a dysfunctional body that relies on a cane or a wheelchair isn't even a little white lie because there is no question about that. Later for confidential revelations.

I submit my profiled aliased photoless self and within hours I become a non-fetish submissive, a prisoner to the habit of checking for responses obsessively. And lo and behold, if they don't come and keep coming. But after three or four weeks and a few dozen people requesting emails, before I even seriously contemplate opening communication lines, I notice a trend. The mature males like Bob from Lac la Biche, and Canucklehead from Surrey and Rod from Null all want to spend time in their boy toys with an able-bodied adventuress and every first date suggestion is a walk on the beach or dinner and a movie which makes me rethink disability honesty.

So okay. The normal dating channels are not open to me. I admit to a certain degree of failure.

But hang on. Here's a disability dating site. This could be for me! The only obstacle is that there are 325 conditions/diseases/flaws to choose from. So here's a new problem. Do I make a selection by my disease? I suppose it would make sense to share common problems as a way to break down that first big barrier but maybe a mixed-disease "relationship" would be more interesting. You'd have differences rather than commonalities to talk about. Before or after the sex part. What to do, what to do!

Wait a minute. What's this? Google still rules. Here's a site where I can have simulated sex and closer than third-party stimulation. Create my own scenario by schematic. I can choose by themed room or outdoors Garden of Eden or circus. Circus! I can choose my own alter-body, all fit, trim, and even able. All I need to do is purchase a membership and the sexual enhancement tool that plugs into my computer and emulates the sensations of my own personal character's activities on the screen. But my credit card is in denial. It's a no-go. And the wind in the treetops has picked up to gale-force magnitude.

If I were braver, I could just build my own website advertising the fact that I have three orgasms left and I need a trio of hearty, sensual souls to rise to the occasion. I could have a TV reality show with games and competitions on the Showcase channel, just like Jerry Hall, or Flava Flav or *Survivor*, with a cash prize generated from membership and application fees just like a literary contest. I could market mugs and hats and brand-name anything. But I'd need an assistant for the business end of things and a decade. And within weeks, I'd have to defend my site from copycats. Such complications. But what if the cash wasn't big enough to entice anyone and there would be the public photo issue again.

This is defeating, weird, frustrating, and do I dare say the D-word, depressing. Gawd, now I need a twelve-step program to battle this addictive online dating business. And I haven't even answered an email or posted on a blog or talked to anyone in a chat room.

I need a break. No, I have to stop.

I pull up confessions-online and type in: I am a hedonist, a deviant, and I am an internet dating site addict.

That's when it hits. A great crash, total darkness, a blank screen. It must have been a tree coming down on the roof. I hear the howl of wind and slashing rain. No white noise, no refrigerator running or radio hum or electric heater. But there is no gaping hole in the roof. I do what any survivor of addiction does. I find my wheelchair, a flashlight, two extra blankets, my cell phone (which has slipped out of the service area all by itself) and go to bed. I did it. I turned my still-solitary back to the blank screen without another hopeful glance. Without tomorrow's horoscope, or tea-leaf reading, or even a finished submitted online confession. I slide my maxed-out credit card under my pillow and for the first time in days, I dream of absolutely nothing.

Liberation

October is my favourite time of year. The heat of summer is a distant memory and rain arrives on my doorstep more frequently than any other visitor. I like the solitude, enforced confinement—until I hate it. And it's only the first of the month. And a Friday to boot, so a weekend of isolation and empty arms is hovering on the horizon.

I've ditched my buddy (the cane) for new best friends: my wheelchair (a previous acquaintance) and a motorized scooter. There's a limit to how many times I can fall without reaching the breaking point and I'm approaching that limit at a rapid pace. Black and blue are the most disconcerting colours.

Besides, it's only the really old guys who check out my equipment—mechanical or otherwise. Needless to say, my rating on the desirability scale is bottoming out faster than my rising number on the disability scale, which is threatening 6.5 out of a probable and eventual 10. But, disability and desirability are both "d" words with a difference of "e" and "r" and if you put those three letters together you get red, which leads to my latest equipment purchase. My new crimson underwire is the most uplifting thing in my life these days, but if I don't show it to somebody soon, it's gonna fray or kink or something worse, like ending up in a bag for Value Village.

This whole orgasm thing has me by the nonexistent balls. It's not the only problem, obviously, but I'm sick and tired of researching sick and tired. Plus, I can't concentrate on anything else. At all. And deeper issues like world peace or even my personal future take a back seat to the orgasms. Three. If I could resolve this satisfactorily, I'm convinced I could actually get on with the rest of my limited life. Maybe even write a poem or two. Close the steamy carnal chapter, so to speak.

I need a refined plan. Step by step. So I get busy. And procrastinate. I'm pretty sure if I wait too long I'll lose the option of any more orgasms, but I rationalize that they're always more eventful, bigger and better, after a sexual dry spell. And I'm bloody well parched. I have to space them out, and although each one may work up to fruition over a series of episodes, I'm ultimately looking for three different participants. Or situations. Or planes of sensual consciousness.

Everyone needs a discipline, so I attach myself to the number three—another curvy numeral—until I can adopt another field of interest that's nonsexual. Fortitude and tenacity, even I can manage short term, hopefully without getting nasty.

I look up old boyfriends on Facebook because nothing else on the internet has worked out. I find a couple, but their status reads Married. I'm just not that into the complications of that. There's a message from my old friend John, who promises to stop by for a beer if I'm up to it. He'll be in the neighbourhood. Thursday, he says. The seventh, I think, which is six days from now (two times three), so I message back, fine. At least he'll be company of the male variety for a couple of hours. He'll probably regale me with tales of his latest nymphomaniac girlfriend. Perfect. Not.

In the meantime, I figure I'll make myself presentable and available every three days for the month of October, which gives me eleven hot opportunities (including today, and ending on Hallowe'en for a "no holds barred" wild possibility) to bring about a successful outcome. Three orgasms out of eleven attempts make for decently optimistic odds. Better than pi, in fact, and even better than a vulgar (technically, I kid you not) fraction like .33333. While I'm not exactly lazy, I get overwhelmed with the preparation for and execution of social contact. Still, I'm ready, really ready to put myself out there. In order to avoid utter exhaustion I am allowing myself two days between each foray to chill out, make crisp notes, make myself cool all over again. If things work out ahead of time, all the better. Like by Thanksgiving.

I ask the universe to assist me, maybe even give me a sign. Sure as guns, in a matter of minutes, three ravens swoop through the scant trees across the way. Okay, that's not true. But I do find three hangnails on my left hand while I'm waiting for the miraculous sign. Then it happens. I get three text messages. They're from a number I don't recognize but it contains three threes and is local. The spelling's not so hot but the spell works.

>   *Hey*, reads the first.
>   The next is a little more interesting.
>   *Im softly kissing your neck*
>   And, oh my.
>   *Now slowly moveing down your body. Nibbbling*
>   I can't help but notice three Bs.

I figure this is a way better sign than the hangnails, regardless of the fact that the words aren't meant for me. After all, technology is a big part of our universe. And then there was that weird call last Xmas that turned out to be for Marvin and his magical thumbs, even before I'd ever met him. I do a reverse search in 411 but it's a cell number so there's no listing. I think this stranger must have realized my number isn't the right number. I wait, half-thankful half-disappointed. I give up, light a cigarette, thinking about places to meet people. There are three more texts. I finish my smoke, then open one every three minutes although it takes less time for them to arrive. Anticipation rocks.

>   *working side to side down your body with muy*

I realize that the texts are character-limited and/or the sender is also an anticipation-appreciator.

>   *tongue to your inner thigh kissing softly every now and than*

I'm kind of speechless, a little flushed even.
One side then the other working to the middle where I blow softly
Then nothing. It's okay. While I cool off, I save the number in my contacts just in case there's a desperate need for further communication and I have the guts to text back.

Anything is possible and nothing is off limits, including the equipment-checking old guys, so I charge up my scooter, which happens to have three wheels. Bingo. Maybe that's a good place to start—all those daubers and balls and numbers. Plus the fact that the number three key on a phone also stands for "D," "E," and "F" so now I know I should look for somebody hearing-impaired and if they're at the local bingo hall, they'll probably have functional hearing aids.

It's time to get excited. So I begin. I make a list of possible situations for meeting people, aside from Craig's List and internet options—triads, trios, and threesomes, which take on their own naughty triangular "Yvon(n)ic" connotations. And counting to three often signals some synchronous act, like one, two, three—pull! Or one, two, three—open your eyes! Or one, two, three—jump! Rock paper scissors may dictate the order.

1. *Three wishes* turbaned genie (maybe?)
2. *Three witches in Shakespeare's* Macbeth (undecided)
3. *Three strikes, you're out* (where I'm looking to be)
4. *Three strikes in bowling, called a turkey* (Thanksgiving holds promise)
5. *Three bears* (hairy guys?!)
6. *Three little pigs* (straw, wood?! brick, maybe carpenters?)
7. *Three blind mice* (if the deaf situation doesn't work out)
8. *Three stooges* (Comedy Club?)
9. *Roman numeral III* (all upright, phallic)
10. *Triathlon: swimming, biking, running* (I could be a spectator??)

11. Primary colours, including red, my favourite
Bonus ***12. Three means life in Chinese culture
Extra Bonus 13. Third time lucky !!!

The community hall is about three blocks down the street, just within scooter distance, which is important as I have to be able to get back home without the battery going dead. This is the same hall that holds Fetish Night once a month, so I wonder if I'll find any souvenirs.

I put on some lipstick and head to Bingo Heaven early so I have time to get my bearings without baring anything. Yet. The atmosphere leaves something to be desired—long folding tables, only twenty people so far, but others follow me in. I look for attractions and hearing aids while I purchase a paltry four bingo sheets, but end up sitting alone at a table, leaving the universe in charge.

It isn't long before several serious aficionados pull up their chairs. The woman beside me in long black leather seems overdressed, out of place, but is all business. She arranges thirty or so sheets and a rainbow of ink daubers while I wonder if she also attends monthly get-togethers here with her own version of specialty equipment. I take note of her large frame and bleached blond hair. No hearing aids but I have to repeat every technical Bingo question twice, so maybe she needs them. I can't guess her age. Somewhere between young and old. Like me.

As the games proceed and the jackpot continues to grow, I find myself falling behind and my black leather neighbour leaning in to help. She's quick and practiced and I don't mind a bit cuz the jackpot I'm after isn't monetary. She seems to be touching my arm a lot, gently nudging me when I miss the numbers, which are sadly lacking in the three department. Blondie wears three serious silver rings, those extended knuckle ones with hinges. When it's done she's won several times and I've won nothing. We haven't even exchanged names, but she suggests coffee and she'll buy.

It turns out coffee doesn't mean a cozy café but the back corner of the local Starbucks patio, which is really chilly but we can smoke. She sits close, a little too close even for me, who's not feeling much in the erotic department. We clutch our über-hot paper coffee cups. It isn't 'til I find her mouth on mine that I think the night may not be a total bust after all.

"Let's walk," she says.

"Not much of an option," I reply, finding it so odd that people forget to pay attention.

"Well, we can't do much here."

"What do you have in mind?"

She doesn't reply but pulls out her multi-coloured bingo daubers and draws a red arrow on the palm of my hand. It feels kinda weird, cool and moist.

"It's washable," she says, loosening the cotton scarf around my neck and draws in blue what I figure to be an arrow from my ear down my throat ending in my red satin-clad excuse for a cleavage. I'm not sure what to do, so I do nothing.

Her eyes scan the empty patio and the lit interior. There's another kiss. No, more than a kiss. A nibble. No, more than a nibble. Her lips are on my throat. And her teeth. A nip. No, not a nip. A small bite.

"Bite me or I'll bite you harder," she hisses, pulling my head to her. I can't get away. I consider pleading but the whole thing is weird enough to turn me on a little.

I try to pull away, thinking fear, thinking scream, thinking run, which is not an option. I'm stuck with fight over flight but I'm not good at that either. I think friendly (sort of) biting beats out fighting. So I nibble just a little. She nips at my lips and throat and ear lobe. I don't know if it's the biting or the chilly October evening, but I'm all shivery. I'm feeling tender, my skin, not my heart. The only thing I'm sure of is the urgent need for a getaway. Now. My coffee cup flips its lid thanks to the nimble fingers on my good hand and spills just enough to make her jerk away. I boot the scooter inside, where the evil-eyed barista calls me a cab—a wheelchair one that'll take an hour. I say that's fine. I'll wait. I hold my breath, not wanting to look in the direction of the patio. Then I look. There's no one there. No coffee cup. No spills. I convince myself I'm delusional, that it never happened, that multiple vampire movies have had a detrimental effect on me.

As the cabby, named Ivan, buckles and straps me and my scooter safely in, I find my voice, the semi-sultry one, and proving to myself I'm not really rattled and am still on task, I say, "I love it when you do that." Neither of us speaks on the short drive. He's got another fare waiting. Too bad. He ramps me out and I pay and tip and smile and he smiles back.

"Another time," he says with a mock salute. I notice an over-toothy glint.

I go straight to the bathroom. If I couldn't see proof in the mirror and feel the fine necklace of angry little bite marks at my throat, I'd still believe it was my imagination playing tricks although it's nowhere close to Hallowe'en. And the coloured arrows are still there. Waterproof, it seems. I scrub and cringe and scrub until my skin's as red as my bra. I apply calendula oil to ease the inflammation because it's October's birth flower, it's often yellow (another primary colour), and it has nine (three-squared) lucky letters. No blood was drawn, but my scant (thankfully) period has arrived, making a sneak preview. Lovely. I lock up my doors and my libido and chow down on Lay's chips 'n garlic dip.

I recuperate for two days and on the fourth of the month I peruse my somewhat trusty list. I decide Marvin may actually have been the genie sans the turban but with magic thumbs so I cross out number one. Number two I figure must have been the Bingo witch, considering there was semi-boiling liquid involved and a lot of toil and trouble to make my getaway. Number three, the strikes, hopefully means baseball, unless someone's just striking matches instead of Bics, which could be anywhere with cigarettes or woodstoves or candles. Or, gawd forbid, unlikely-in-Canada air strikes involving fighter jets. But none of them reach speeds yet of Mach 3, so that idea's blown out of the water. I'll play it a little safer this time. Cruise the neighbourhood in my car. Yes, I still drive. With wheelchair and scooter on board—my reinforcements.

I cover up the string of marks on my throat with makeup and a turtleneck sweater. The baseball diamonds are empty but for a few soccer players cuz, of course, it's October. I follow a drift of wood smoke to a backyard bonfire but I haven't been invited and it looks to be far too family-oriented for my mission. I consider a bar down the road with a smoking stone chimney, but I have a feeling I need to find somebody who can stay awake long enough to ensure success, just in case it's gonna be harder, uh, more difficult to actually reach a climax. Niagra might be a handy thing to have around and I don't mean the waterfalls although I'm aware discharge can be ballistically copious. Plus the pills are blue, the last primary colour. I go home slightly deflated, but order little blue pills on the internet, with a three-day delivery guarantee.

Three days later, after my special delivery, my phone rings. I hope it's the amorous texter but, no, it's John.

"Hey, Mel. How's tricks?"

"Nonexistent," I say, half thinking that turning a few might be an option. "Don't tell me. You're not coming."

"Uh, I'm not coming."

"Jeezus, John, you ... "

"Kidding. Just kidding. You're touchy."

"Yeah, well ... "

"Beer and hockey sound okay? I'll even bring a pizza."

"Hey, that actually sounds good. Like old times."

"Puck drops in an hour. See you then."

I make adjustments to my list, erasing the witches, replacing *triathlon* with *hat trick*, and crossing out a few more while I'm at it. What the hell. Maybe I will just put it to him—my dilemma.

~~1. Three wishes turbaned genie (maybe?)~~

~~3. Three strikes, you're out (where I'm looking to be)~~

4. *Three strikes in bowling, called a turkey* (Thanksgiving holds promise)

5. *Three bears* (hairy guys?!)

6. *Three little pigs* (straw, wood?! brick, maybe carpenters?)

7. *Three blind mice* (if the deaf situation doesn't work out)

8. *Three stooges* (Comedy Club?)

9. *Roman numeral III* (all upright, phallic)

~~10. Triathlon: swimming, biking, running (I could be a spectator??)~~ Hat trick (hockey)

~~11. Primary colours, including red, my favourite~~

Bonus ****12. Three means life in Chinese culture*

Extra Bonus 13. *Third time lucky !!!*

"You seem preoccupied," says John later, already three beers and half a pizza into the game. Third period's coming up and the Canuckleheads are down 3–2.

"Really? Sorry."

There's a news flash about the Chilean miners—33 of them rescued after 69 days underground. It's another numerical miracle, but the gravity of their situation, their near demise, makes me feel bad, really bad, as well as shallow and narcissistic.

"Wanna talk?" John asks, settling back like I'm going to hit him with something mentally heavy.

"Talking is the last thing on my mind."

"Meaning?"

"Meaning I don't want to talk." I'm all agitated. Pouty.

"Okay. Well what do you wanna do? We've got fifteen minutes."

"What I want to do is have a hat trick." Preoccupied is an understatement. I am cranky and even if John was somebody else (which he's not), fifteen minutes would not be enough. I mean really!

"You might be in luck. Sedin's on his way."

"No, John. Not Sedin. Me. Before I'm sent down to the farm team." And with that, I dissolve into tears. Pathetic blubbery tears that demand a hug. At least a hug. And I get it, because John has no idea what else to do. He pulls me close, attempting to calm me, diffuse the baffling emotional situation. I comply, wiping my nose on his shirt. It's all comfy there and so soothing—the aftershave, the warmth, his hands resting against my back. But that's it. I'm in a fix and comfy just isn't going to cut it.

"Kleenex," I say.

John passes me the box looking simultaneously concerned and relieved, just waiting. For me to compose myself. For the third period to start. For a return to normalcy.

"Phew. Enough of that."

John pats my knee. "Any time you wanna talk."

"Thanks," I say, knowing my desperate sexual situation is not appropriate or comfortable or smart to discuss. I also know the differences between men's and women's listening skills and which part of the conversation to take seriously, especially when hockey's involved. I know what he's thinking, that it's the MS thing, which is a perfectly acceptable excuse for tears in John's books.

Sedin fails at the hat trick. So do I. For now. I feel better after my teary little episode though—all that self-pity flushed out. A fresh slate. I even manage a mysterious smile when I admit I've got plans for Thanksgiving that don't include him or Charlene or even Jackie. I keep my plans secret. Even from myself.

We hug goodnight, mutually reassuring. There is not one iota of spark. I'll save that for some unsuspecting turkey on the tenth. The 10th! 10/10/10! Three tens cannot be anything but lucky, considering it's a symbol of perfection, and in temporal binary it equals 42, which is, of course, divisible by three.

Again, I ready myself—get a little dolled up. Between hair and makeup, I text the mystery texter with three quick before-I-change-my-mind messages, allowing for slightly more honesty than I can muster with friends, acquaintances, or medical professionals.

recruiting volunteers to have sex with hot disabled chick
position open immediately
sliding pay scale

Promiscuity and sluttiness cannot be considered as drawbacks when faced with dire straits, or straights. I don't expect a response anyway, but have fun sending the texts. It's not even a novel idea—the volunteers. They're already doing it in Switzerland.

In the meantime, the bar may have to suffice for doable options, which would work, seeing as I have backup pills to fortify someone's drink if need be. The problem with this is sitting alone in a bar on a sentimental statutory holiday. So I go early, mid-afternoon as though I have somewhere else familial to be later. It's dead but for a few late-lunchers and a couple of sadsack permanent bachelors, until the boys roll in from the Rod 'n Gun Club turkey shoot all plaid-clad and jovial. A couple of them that I know a little pull up bragging chairs, happy to talk buckshot. I'm willing enough to listen, question even, waiting for a sign from somebody, almost anybody.

There's one particularly dark furry guy who's got curly chest hairs spilling out over his Stanfields, which could be a good sign for the three bears on my list. But he also has hair on the back of his hands, which filters down to a bare white patch on his ring finger where a ring should be nestled pointing symbolically to an inevitable turkey dinner with kids and grandparents. The other is too young and too sweet-faced, even for me. So when they leave, I'm not overly disappointed. Resigned is more like it. But wait, what's this? Another man, quietly asking if he can sit here.

Tom's not unattractive by any stretch, which makes me a lot hot and a little suspicious, but there are no obvious signs of marriage about him. In fact, he admits sheepishly he's single again in the girlfriend department and that he's noticed me in here before. And not because of the wheelchair, he's quick to point out. He's younger than he sounds and older than he looks. He wears glasses, which are such a turn-on lately and there's not one thing mousy about him. He's in no hurry, it seems, so we have a couple of drinks, order hot turkey sandwiches after I lie, falsely admit not wanting to go to my family dinner and give thanks properly. He talks dogs. And carpentry. Straw, wood, or brick, I ask. All three have their advantages, he says. One more drink and the conversation drifts around to disease, mine. And then desire, everybody's. I mention the Swiss volunteer experiment and he gets a funny look on his face, digs out his cell phone, presses a couple of buttons, and lays it open on the table between us. I swear the thing is smoking.

He heads to the Keno machine, leaving me there to think or maybe he's daring me to check out his tauntingly open phone but I don't need to. Okay, I can't help it. I do need to. Yup. There's my text on his phone starting with *position open immediately.* There's no point in blushing or apologies. I crush half a pill into his drink and stir things up before he returns.

"Well then ... " I say.

"Speaking of positions ... " he says.

"Mmhmm ... "

"Straw, wood, or brick?"

"All three ... " I say, resting my hand on his thigh, "in a row."

"Now?"

"Oh, yeah. Home with me. You follow."

He's big enough (all over, I hope, checking out his promising boots) to lift me out of the van and carry me to the patio. The kiss is also promising. Not overly romantic. All animal, in this situation, is just fine with me. No, not fine. Preferable. No not preferable. Necessary.

He lets me lead and we just get down to juicy business, bits of clothing still on (my favourite), right there on the brick patio. Chaise lounges come in handy for more than suntanning. He's downright delicious and I'm close to sexual resolution, but not quite, so we move out of the invigorating October chill into the warm house and find ourselves on the rattan rug, which I equate to straw. I'm teetering on the brink, but he beats me to it. No!

"I just need a fiver," he huffs (and puffs).

"This isn't a fuck 'n run, is it? I hate that."

"Well, I really shouldn't be driving," he admits.

"Bed, then," I say, as I motion toward my bedroom, and my wooden four-poster.

"You're something else." He gives his head a shake, and I let him think it's all me, not the pharmaceuticals.

Thankfully, we don't talk much. Leave the lights on (my call). I let him get his wind. When he starts asking unusual-for-a-one-nighter questions like when was the last time you had sex, do you like porn, and why do you like sheets, I cover his lips with mine and off we go again. And this time, it works. Really effing works, like effing-tastic and effing-nomenal and effing-tasmagorical. I don't mind the excessive dampness everywhere. He's warm and sleepy and soon unmoving. And me, I feign sleep enjoying the feel and smell and sight of him. And the fact that I'm not only very satisfied physically but also mentally. Yes, I still have it (whatever it is) and yes, I'll be done with this whole fairy tale soon.

Lights out and I drift finally. Sleep is another beautiful thing.

Dreaming, too. I press replay over and over. Yum. Geez, it seems so real that when I wake up I think I'm almost coming all over again. It seems so real, I can still smell and feel and see him. And then, oh. What's happening is, um, really real. He's all tucked in behind me, and is having a slow-rolling half-awake morning effing-screw. With sleepy dreamy me. And, oh my, I'm apparently having an effing-screw back. And it's good. Really good. Oh, eff it. The universe rules even in sleep. So I give in to it. Totally. My-oh-effing-my!

"Enjoy your day," Tom says, on leaving. I enjoyed every minute of him, which is the way things should be before they end. Watching him dress was equally as good as the previous night's opposite. This brings my mind only briefly to the number 2. Good and evil. Hot and cold. Pairs and pears, cuz now that my second to last orgasm has been used up, I'm incredibly hungry for sweet curvy October fruit.

Three Dog Night sings on the radio "One is the loneliest number." I wish I'd added that to my three-list, but it's too late now. I'm down to *one*—an orgasm number I refuse to spend alone. Number one also means goodbye, which is what I'll happily say to sex soon. Dear gawd, it's excruciatingly hard work just keeping up sexy desirable appearances. But I'm not done just yet. I still have my list—the one that needs serious updating. I cross out bears, mice, and little pigs. It's getting pretty skimpy.

~~1. Three wishes turbaned genie (maybe?)~~

~~3. Three strikes, you're out (where I'm looking to be)~~
~~4. Three strikes in bowling, called a turkey (Thanksgiving holds promise)~~
~~5. Three bears (hairy guys?!)~~
~~6. Three little pigs (straw, wood?! brick, maybe carpenters?)~~
~~7. Three blind mice (if the deaf situation doesn't work out)~~

8. *Three stooges* (Comedy Club?)
9. *Roman numeral III* (all upright, phallic)
~~10. Triathlon: swimming, biking, running (I could be a spectator??) Hat trick (hockey)~~
~~11. Primary colours, including red, my favourite~~
Bonus ****12*. Three means life in Chinese culture
Extra Bonus 13. Third time lucky !!!

I figure I should scope out Roman noses or somebody with a wicked sense of humour or both. Noses can be as telltale as feet, I've heard, so someone with a ponderous protrusion who can remember jokes (unlike myself) should fit the bill and foot it, to boot, although I won't hold them to the paying part.

One's not a bad number, in Roman numerals or otherwise. I like the shape. Pure simplicity—like a bullet, which I'm more than a little prepared to bite for the sake of freedom, or liberation, or even deliverance from this numerological blessing-curse. And it symbolizes so many apropos characteristics for my final climactic act—urgency for new beginnings, action (both mental and physical), positivity, and strong will. And I read somewhere that if one urges us to some pure urgent natural action, we'll be rewarded in kind. Tit for tat, in a good way.

Every one of my senses has been heightened since turkey day. Tom was a terrific semi-finalist—a runner-up with the mostest who helped me out more than he knew. Now, it's on to bigger, better, more final things.

I look in my closet, thinking a dress is called for, nothing bridal but the opposite of that, black. No, not black. Too funereal, and it makes me look sallow. Red, then. Again. But with black boots. Biggest earrings ever. I make sure I have cash in my wallet in case I have to pay for the privilege of achieving Numero Uno.

I can't decide where to go, to look, to hook up. It's a real issue.

I could call a cab and ask the driver, but the cabbie the other night is too toothy and creepy-night-associated. But they do know where to find any and every thing. I can't afford to stall so I call, checking to see who's on tonight for the handi-van. It's not Ivan, which is good but the wait'll be over an hour, which is bad. Now I have time to waste.

I twiddle my thumbs, check my nails, reapply lipstick. I could use a sign right about now. Something ethereal. Nothing happens. It's too quiet for my nervous tension. I turn on the TV.

It's the news. More about the reborn Chilean miners, more about hockey, more about modern medicine. I wait for it wondering if it'll be about botoxing your G-spot or your bladder or maybe cosmetic surgery for your genitals. But, hey, this is about multiple sclerosis. I've heard or tried everything there is to hear or try. It's another theory but this one is procedural rather than medicinal.

They're talking about a small Italian study with remarkable results and referencing before and after clips of MSers showing improvement. Some remain static, like no progression, while others are better. The story's not that exciting until it suddenly is.

They're calling it "Liberation"—this angioplasty. Just a minor incision, a catheter, and poof, they balloon open narrowed areas in the veins, like jugulars. Apparently, the blocked or narrowed veins have been preventing excess iron in the brain from draining away. I like the idea. No toxic drugs. No injections. No hopeless.

I'll believe it when I see it, but I really want to see it or see about it at least. I boot up the computer. Holy crap. Liberation is everywhere. It's going viral. They're already doing it in Poland and India and Egypt and other medical tourism hotspots in Central America, like Costa Rica and Panama. Not in Canada though. Oh no. Far too experimental. But life is one long (hopefully) experiment. I dig and research and read and research until I'm nearly cross-eyed. Screw the orgasm dilemma. This might be even bigger. Like health, or something closer to that. Imagine.

There's a knock at the door.

"What?" I call, totally put out at the interruption. "Who ... is it?"

I hear a muffled voice, a man's voice.

"Oh, shit. Just a minute."

I wheel to the door, open it a little and see a darn nice-looking fella. I open the door a little wider, taking a good look.

"You called a cab?" he asks.

Well, well, I think. But what I say is, "A cab? No I did not call a cab. Must be some mistake." I shut the door on the puzzled good-looker. He knocks again. I don't answer, hear his receding footsteps and spinning gravel as the taxi peels away.

I get right back to the computer where I slip off my earrings, stockings, and special-occasion garter belt. Down to business. I crumple the old list and toss it somewhere random behind me.

I fill out applications for three countries, all thankfully online. It's incredibly expensive—in the thousands, which is way out of my reach but I'll worry about that later. Fundraise, or beg Charlene. The possibilities are endless. I'll make a list. But first I think about my life, its style, that is, and what I can quit like drinking, smoking, and being a couch (wheelchair) potato.

And then I have a scary thought. What if ... what if my orgasm limit goes up? Well, I can't really waste time right now thinking about that. I have things to do. And I'll take it one orgasm, uh, I mean one day at a time.

I get the call on the thirteenth, a seriously lucky number. I have a date with Costa. Costa Rica, that is, and I can't wait.

Acknowledgements

Kudos and gratitude to Vici Johnstone of Caitlin Press, for your support and faith in my writing, and to my editor, Meg Taylor, who possesses just the right kind of wonderful and knows how to use it.

Heartfelt thanks to my family and friends and especially my kids, who continue to inspire, nudge, and cajole me on my writerly journey, both in my presence and absence.

Thank you to my writing group peers—particularly Rebecca Hendry, Erin Whalen, and Diane Foley—for your open-minded sharp-eyed critiques, unrelenting enthusiasm, and humour. Special thanks to Betty Keller, mentor extraordinaire. Couldn't have done it without you!

Much appreciation to my first creative writing instructor, Ryan Knighton, for cracking open the stubborn literary door, to my last creative writing instructor, Marilyn Bowering, for knocking that door off its hinges, and all those in between.

A non-fiction excerpt from Chapter Two in "Six Degrees of Altered Sensation" was published in *Body Breakdowns: Tales of Illness and Recovery*, edited by Janis Harper (Toronto: Anvil Press, 2007).

"Dick & Jane & the Barbecue" was published as "Dick & Jane & the Barbecue, and, No, It's Not a Love Story" in the *scratch 2010 anthology VOLUME 3: short stories and poetry* http://www.scratch-contest.net

Kim Clark lives on Vancouver Island. Disease and desire, mothering and the mundane propel her ongoing journey between poetry and prose. Kim's work can be found in *Body Breakdowns* (Anvil Press), the *Malahat Review*, e-zines and other publications in Canada and the US. She was a 2010 winner in the scratch Poetry and Fiction Contests and was short-listed in the *Malahat Review* 2010 Novella Contest. Kim holds a BA in Creative Writing from Vancouver Island University and has edited for Artistry and Portal. *Attemptations* is her first book.